T0354911

ISLAND OF THE PORTAL

ISLAND
P OF THE ORTAL

E. THORNTON GOODE, JR.

ISLAND OF THE PORTAL

iUniverse books may be ordered through booksellers or by contacting:

iUniverse
1663 Liberty Drive
Bloomington, IN 47403
www.iuniverse.com
844-349-9409

ISBN: 978-1-6632-6135-9 (sc)
ISBN: 978-1-6632-6136-6 (e)

Library of Congress Control Number: 2024905646

Print information available on the last page.

iUniverse rev. date: 04/16/2024

In Appreciation

I want to thank my friend, Galen Berry, for helping with the proofreading and editing process. He always makes excellent suggestions to improve and enhance the storylines of my novels. This is the ninth book he has helped me with. In this novel, he also has allowed me to use his picture to represent the character, Mark Lancaster. Thank you, Galen, for all your help both past and present.

Julian Green is the perfect representation for the image of Brody Hollister in the story. Thank you, Julian. I miss you so very much. You continue to live on in my heart and in my writings.

Galen

Happenstance

Julian

Bio Information

Living in Mexico is wonderful. Being retired, I have time to do the things I want to do. There are no schedules, timetables and the like.

This is my thirteenth novel going to print. It's the last one so far. I haven't had an inspiration for a new novel in recent times. Some say it's writer's block. Maybe my imagination is dead. We shall see. Time will tell.

Because the publisher of my first two novels has gone out of business, I am going to have my current publisher republish those books, so they will be available to readers. I hope to get this done by the end of 2024. We shall see.

After this one is in print, I will be working on getting my short stories published as a collection. I just hope I don't drop dead before I get it done. Yes, I'm laughing.

If this does happen to be my last novel in print, I want to thank all of you who have read some of my books. I hope you have enjoyed the storylines.

Prologue

Are you one of those people who likes to have everything planned out, orderly and running smoothly? To be honest, I try my damnedest to do the best I can but it doesn't always work out that way. Regardless of what I do, something usually comes up, making me have to do some kind of correction. But this is usually with the small things.

Now, with life-altering, important things, I've tried to be diligent. I've tried to think of the future and make arrangements for it. A good example of this was saving for retirement.

Many laugh and think it's eons away. Guess what? It isn't. It's right around the corner. So, instead of taking the money you would waste on some moronic thing, you should buy some stock, even if it's only one share. Especially, if it pays a dividend. Got it? Forget about a savings account. Bank interest rates suck.

I was one who waited very late, almost too late and had to scramble at the last minute. Yes, I was fifty-six when I finally woke up and smelled the coffee. I started taking every extra dollar and buying stock. I was also fortunate the stocks I bought were good ones and paid dividends which I turned right around and reinvested.

In the beginning, I wasn't stupid. Two years out of graduate school, I bought a house. Not only did I buy a house but fortunately enough, it was in an area that eventually boomed because of its excellent school system. Everyone with kids wanted to be in that area. I was lucky. I do attribute it to the Fates stepping in. So, the house I bought in 1971 for a little over twenty-two thousand dollars sold in 2013 for three hundred and five thousand. Yep. I had some decent capital for beginning my retirement. What can I say?

Sale of the house allowed me to begin a pretty good retirement on top of my Social Security check, the dividends from the stocks I bought and a small pension from the first company I worked for after grad school. Another thing that helped significantly big time at retirement is that I moved. Living where I'd been was way too expensive. Property taxes alone there were insane. The house was just twelve hundred square feet. Did you get that? Twelve hundred square feet. The property taxes were just over five thousand dollars a year and the city was about to raise them to around seven thousand five hundred dollars a year. Paying the property taxes alone would have taken virtually half of my annual Social Security.

Now, let me tell you what I did to solve that crisis. I bought a three-quarter-acre lot, four hundred and fifty feet from the ocean, built a house that is six hundred square feet larger than the one I sold and I'm happy as a clam. The lot was seventy-five thousand dollars. That's right. Seventy-five thousand. Property taxes are two hundred dollars a year. Correct. And it's summer all the time which means no heating bills. So, where is this wonderful inexpensive place? It's on the southwest coast of Mexico some fifty miles up the coast from Zihuatanejo. My retirement dollars go a very long way here.

Now, my question to you is this. Are you prepared?

The character in this story was on top of everything to be prepared. He'd taken everything into account. He knew a rainy day could come along and he wanted to be set and ready for it. He even had backup plans in case plan 'A' didn't work out right. Retirement? He was ready by his late thirties. Nothing could go wrong. All the bases were covered. He was ready. His retirement would be a breeze.

Little did he know that the Fates and Destiny were going to step in and throw him a curveball. He was going to be faced with something for which he could never have planned. Something right out of left field. The event to occur would be life-altering in more ways than one.

Chapter I

"'Call me Ishmael.' No! No! Just kidding. Just kidding! That's not really my name. I just wanted to one day start a story like that. My apologies to Herman Melville. Actually, my name is irrelevant. No..... my name is NOT... 'Irrelevant'. Geez. It's because names aren't that important in this story. They're just a way of sorting who everyone is. Okay. My name is really Mark. Mark Lancaster. Are you satisfied? Yeah."

But there aren't many characters in this story to try and keep them apart. I mean, this is NOT... <u>War</u> <u>and</u> <u>Peace</u> where it's impossible to remember who the hell is who in probably the longest damn novel ever written. What can I say? I think when I finally meet Tolstoy in the Great Beyond, I'm going to beat the shit out of him. Once for each of his damn characters. Something tells me that I'll possibly have to stand in line. When I say that, in my head, I see the wonderful scene in the movie, 'Airplane'. You know, where all the passengers are lined up in the aisle, ready to beat the shit out of another passenger. Damn, I love that scene. I roar with laughter every time I see it. "So, Tolstoy! You BITCH! Watch out! We're coming for you."

It's funny, thinking about using the first line of <u>Moby</u> <u>Dick</u> for my story. Just as in that book, the ocean is a significant part of mine. I love the ocean. I love the beach and always have. But I have great respect for the ocean. It can be your friend one moment but it can also be a terror the next. There's a line from a song by Lee Ann Womack. The song is *I Hope You Dance* and the line is, 'I hope you still feel small when you stand beside the ocean.' To me, anyone who doesn't feel small when they stand beside the ocean is an egotistical bastard, probably with a God complex. I try to steer clear of folks like that.

Okay. Sorry for the diversion. Now, where was I? Yes. Trying to get this story started. So, here goes. 'It was the best of times. It was the worst of...' Okay! Okay! Just kidding! Just kidding! I couldn't help it. I couldn't resist. But to be honest, for me, it really was the best of times.

I was happy. My work as an architect for a major firm in Atlanta was going well. I didn't owe the bank too much money and I had a retirement house already built on the southwest coast of Mexico. It was located about fifty miles up the coast from Zihuatanejo. Yes, that town mentioned at the end of the movie, 'The Shawshank Redemption'. It's not a fictitious place. It's very much real and is about halfway between Acapulco and Puerto Vallarta. Lovely place. I love it there.

Yep. Me, with thirty-nine years under my belt and this far along in life, I was seemingly ahead of the game. My future was assured and nothing was standing in the way of happy times ahead. I know you are wondering about my relationship status. Presently, there is no one because I have not met anyone of significance yet. Yes, I have had encounters but no one rang the bell for me. What can I say?

That said, little did I realize the Fates were about to throw a big monkey wrench into the works. The Destiny I had picked out for myself was obviously not the one the Fates had in store for me. Jean de La Fontaine was right when he said, 'A person often meets his Destiny on the road he took trying to avoid it.' There's also a very good book by Scott Peck. The title speaks volumes. <u>The</u> <u>Road</u> <u>Less</u> <u>Traveled</u>. Fantastic book. It's amazing what can be found and happen on the back roads of life. Check out the book. You'll love it.

And so, it was with me. I was on the easy road. No bumps. No ruts. No holes. Everything was perfect... until that day. Yep, I was on my vacation at the house in Mexico. Unbeknownst to me, I was about to end up on that proverbial road less traveled. It was the day I decided to take the boat out sailing. A day that changed everything for my future, my planned Destiny and my life.

Chapter II

I remember my mother saying to me, "Save. Be frugal. Plan ahead. Buy property because they're not making any more land." I did have to chuckle. I knew she wasn't thinking about the islands of Hawaii where the lava pours into the sea, increasing the area every once in a while. GRIN! Sorry, mom.

And so, when I left graduate school and got my first job, I did just as she suggested. I went out and bought a house in October of 1999. It was nice to know I was going to start the new millennium in a house. I was happy about the decision.

Over the next several years, I continued to do the things suggested to me. When I got paid, if there was anything left over after paying the bills, I'd buy stock. It was ridiculous to put any money in a bank savings account. Why? Because the interest rates they were paying weren't even keeping up with inflation. If you put a hundred dollars in your bank's savings account even with the interest by the same time the next year rolled around, it was worth less than the original amount plus the interest. Even though considered as a gamble, stocks seemed to be the way to go, especially stocks paying dividends. And when I'd receive a dividend check, I'd turn right around and reinvest it in more stock. By 2010, everything was looking pretty good.

I knew retirement was still over twenty years in the future. That didn't deter me from thinking about it. I began hearing and reading stories of those moving to foreign countries when they retired. Personally, I wanted to be someplace warm and somewhat tropical. After much investigation, I realized the southwest coast of Mexico offered exactly what I was looking for. Also, there were virtually no hurricanes on the west coast like what would come along on the east coast. And if I wanted to come back to the States for a visit, I didn't have to worry about crossing an ocean. I could even drive if I so desired. Another wonderful advantage was the economy. Nearly everything was cheaper. I did have to consider a little shake from an earthquake every once in a while since that area is sitting next to the 'Ring of Fire'.

By early 2011, I began searching online for real estate agents in the Zihuatanejo area. Almost immediately, I found one. Angelia Martinez. After several emails back and forth, she said she had some property and there was a parcel within my price range. She sent several pictures and short videos to show the property as well as the beach there. I was amazed. It looked perfect. I asked her if she could have the necessary legal papers ready if I came down in October to see the parcel. That wasn't a problem. She said she was looking forward to meeting me.

Of course, now it was essential I get the ball rolling on getting my passport and immigration papers, so I could make the trip.

Question. Have you ever dealt with governmental offices? I swear if a company was run with the efficiency and the kind of employees who work for the government, the company would go bust in no time at all. What a totally frustrating ordeal it is, dealing with them. Oh. And they're NEVER wrong. No. It's always YOUR fault. It was May and they assured me I'd have my passport by the end of June.

You should have seen the expressions on many people's faces when I told them I was going to Mexico in October to buy a lot where I would build my retirement house. Several had to put their hands up over their mouths to hide their snickering. But it was okay. I understood. I've never been able to figure out what it is about people in the United States with their fear of moving to and living in a foreign country. It's not like I was planning to move somewhere in the Middle East. Geez.

I must say, being frugal, investing in stock and owning a house, made my credit score look terrific. I knew exactly how much I needed to borrow to cover the cost of the Mexico lot, the legal fees and the paperwork. Going to the company credit union where I knew virtually everyone there, I had no problem borrowing the money. I used some of my stock as collateral and got a great four percent interest rate.

And my passport? Do you really think it arrived by the end of June? What can I say? I had to call several times. It finally arrived in mid-September.

———— ∿⌀⌀⌀⌀⌀⌀⌀∿ ————

I arrived in Zihuatanejo on Saturday, October 8th. After getting my rental car, I drove directly to the hotel in Troncones. I was to meet Angelia on Monday. The rest of Saturday and all day Sunday I spent by the pool and walking on the beach near the hotel.

———wooeroorooom———

It was around nine-thirty in the morning on Monday when she arrived at the hotel and we drove out to see the property. It was incredible and located about twenty miles up the coast from Troncones. Much better than I thought.

Angelia also explained that getting electricity and digging a well was no problem. I would have to have a cistern built to hold the water I wanted to use. The pump would fill it from the well. In the beginning, I could have the cistern filled by one of the big water trucks that came around. This would give plenty of time to find the right location for a well. It was possible I'd still have to get bottled water to drink as the well water would be suitable for shower and laundry but not for drinking.

That afternoon we went back to the hotel and did all the paperwork. She also suggested a great builder and called him on the phone. He had no problem coming to see me on Tuesday.

Talking to the builder on Tuesday was great. He looked over the architectural drawings for the house and pool I had with me and said it would be no problem to start the coming January. January, 2012. He anticipated it would take around a year to complete. This meant it would be finished in either late January or early February of 2013. I could come down shortly thereafter and start setting up house. There was a very nice cove near the property and I wanted to get a boat to anchor there and use when I was on vacation. Angelia indicated that this was not a problem because virtually all the beach areas in Mexico are owned by the Mexican government, so having a boat in the cove would not be a problem. I would not be trespassing or infringing on someone's personal property.

We both laughed about the pool when the house was so close to the ocean. I told him renters were funny folks. The first question always out of all their mouths was asking if there's a pool. So, it was essential if I planned to do any renting. The placement of the pool also made a very large patio area out in front of the covered terrace directly in front of the house.

After hearing my comment regarding a boat, he said he knew of a very good boat builder and gave me directions to his location in Zihuatanejo. I planned to go see him the next day.

The boat-building man was so cool. He took me around and showed me several nearing completion, so I could see his work. It was obvious he did excellent work.

We sat down and I started explaining the kind of boat I wanted. Just one sail and the mast to be permanently fixed. Also, the boat had to be about eighteen feet long and at least eight feet wide with fairly high sides. I told to him that I have great respect for the ocean and wasn't trying to build some racing boat. I wanted one that would be very stable in the water and not easily tipped over. Its basic use would be for fishing and leisurely outings on the water. I also wanted a nice storage compartment under the back seat area as well as a good-sized one in the front at the bow. I also wanted him to make a lot of nice weatherproof seat cushions, so any guests I had could sit comfortably. They were to have straps, so they could be tied down to prevent them blowing out of the boat from the wind. Several foot-wide boards would be installed just above knee-high and from one side of the boat to the other. These would be the seats for passengers, so they wouldn't have to sit in the bottom of the boat. Since these boards were going to be eight feet long, he indicated he would put a support beam under each one to prevent it from sagging.

He smiled, grabbed a large piece of paper and took a pencil, making a quick drawing. In about ten minutes, he turned the drawing and looked at me. "How do you like this one? I'll put in a support on each side, one for each oar to make rowing easier. On the inside and just above the seats, there will be a rack to hold them when not being used. I'll also put a single seat, a little in front of the mast, to sit on while rowing. Rowing would be done while the sail was down on its support beam. That seat would be placed far enough from the mast, so the person rowing could lean back while rowing and not hit it. That seat would be height-adjustable. It might need to be raised due to the width of the boat and the height of the sides, so the paddles would hit the water." He looked me up and down. "It's possible that you might have to stand."

This made us both laugh.

Then, he asked about a motor for the boat. I told him I didn't want a motor as the upkeep would be ridiculous in the salt atmosphere. If any renters wanted to use the boat during their stay at the house, they would have to realize there was no motor to use in case the wind was not sufficient.

9

He would have a cover made, using stainless steel zippers, so it would go around the mast securely and have snap-flap covers over the zippers. This would prevent any leaks during rainy weather.

I loved it. It was perfect. Giving me a rough idea as to the price, I was quite pleased and told him I'd wire him the money when I got home to Atlanta. I told him he could take his time as I wouldn't be returning until the house was finished. He said it wouldn't be a problem and he'd deliver the boat by the time I arrived next time. He was also going to install a stainless steel post at the beach cove with a long stainless steel chain attached to the post. That way I could lock the boat up, using a stainless steel ring he'd put right on the bow of the boat. He indicated he'd get a lock tolerant of salt air and water to prevent it from rusting. He'd also put a small weather and salt-resistant metal box on top of the post where I could keep the lock and key while the boat was in use. We drew up a contract, shook hands and I left his shop.

For the rest of the time, I drove around, acquainting myself with the area. It was quite obvious the area wasn't like Cancún, Puerto Vallarta, Acapulco or Mazatlán. But I didn't want to be in places like that. I wanted peace, quiet and serenity. I wanted 'Beach in the Country'. And that's exactly what I was getting. I loved it.

———❦———

Needless to say, everyone was totally shocked that I actually went through with my plan of getting property. I think they began to get the picture when I told them I was building a house on the lot and it would probably be finished in a little over a year. When

I wasn't there, I'd rent the house and reinvest that money. And speaking of money, I did have to borrow more and sell some shares to pay for the building of the house and the boat. But I wasn't concerned as I could make enough money renting to pay off the loans and buy more stock.

Yes, the road of my life was perfect. Straight ahead. No bumps. No ruts. No potholes. Just like I planned it.

—————∿∾◦◦⟨⊙⟨⊙⟨⊙◦◦∿—————

The builder was correct. The house was finished in early February of 2013. I came down in March on vacation. The boat builder, knowing I was coming, delivered the boat and anchored it in the cove. He had placed the locking post in the perfect spot. When I saw it, I was extremely pleased. He had locked the boat to the chain and placed the key on the hook that was just inside the door of the house off the covered front terrace. This is where the key would be kept when the boat was not in use. The chain was long enough to reach the ring on the boat with no problems. When the boat was in use, the key would stay in the lock and left in the little box on top of the post.

During my March vacation, I took the boat out several times. It handled exceedingly well. It didn't race through the water but I liked its stability. The rowing seat location and oars were perfect for getting it through the surf before raising the sail. And, yes, I did have to stand and brace myself against the rowing seat and mast while rowing due to my height.

Since I was planning to have renters on a fairly regular basis, it was necessary to install a tower on the back part of the garage in order to have internet and TV reception. This would save a lot of time of having to go into Lázaro Cárdenas to check one's emails, using the internet at one of the coffee shops.

Also, during this visit, I sparsely furnished the house. Just enough to make it comfortable and rentable. Having set up a website when the house got started, I had renters already lined up, beginning in May. I even named the place. Whitby by the Sea. It was in remembrance of the family's old plantation in Virginia back a million years ago... before the 'Recent Unpleasantness', otherwise known as 'the Wowah of Nawthun Aggression'. If you're from the South, I'm sure you got it. GRIN!

Angelia, my real estate lady, agreed to manage and watch over the place when I wasn't there. She got in contact with someone who'd come after each renter and clean up the place for the next one. Angelia said she'd check after each cleaning to make sure a good job was done.

What was also fantastic was Angelia's husband, Carlos, knew about motorcycles. While there, I bought a really nice touring bike. When on vacation, I'd be able to use it for transportation and park it in the garage. Carlos would be able to keep it up and running, during the times I was not around. He would pick me up at the airport in his car, take me to his place to get the bike then I'd use it while on vacation. When time to go home, I'd take it to Carlos, where I'd leave it and he'd take me to the airport in his car. He had a set of keys for the bike in case some glitch happened with coordinating things. Interestingly enough, Carlos also asked if he could do the pool cleaning every week and groundskeeping. It would give him a little extra money as well. I knew he'd do a good job or Angelia would jump all over his ass if he didn't. You bet. It was perfect how everything fell into place.

I set up a bank account just for the house. All rental money would be deposited into that account. I had it so Angelia could pay the property taxes, utilities, the cleaning people, Carlos, maintenance as well as her commission for helping with it all. Also, the monthly loan payment would automatically be withdrawn from that account. This would make it easier for me. I wouldn't have to constantly shift money around to pay the necessities. It would make it considerably easier when it came time to paying income taxes as well. Yep! Life was good and I was happy as a clam. The road was perfectly smooth.

Yes, I can hear you still asking about a significant relationship. I am not someone who rushes into something major. If it's meant to happen, it will. I know I'm thirty-nine years old and not getting any younger. Maybe I was destined to live my life alone.

What can I say? The road I'd planned for my Destiny was both straight and smooth. I was ecstatic. Little did I realize that the Fates had other plans for me. My next vacation in January of 2014 would change everything.

Chapter III

January was a good time to go on vacation in southern Mexico. It was a little cooler than the summer months and also less likely to rain. The rainy season usually started in mid-June and could last into October.

Blocking my two weeks in advance was a good thing because I had renters lined up all the way into September. The money was in the bank. I calculated, even after all the expenses, there would be a tidy sum left over to invest later on.

Angelia told me she was pretty sure more calls would come in from potential renters all the way up to the holidays. She said potential renters loved the website, all the pictures there and were looking forward to vacationing at Whitby by the Sea. Some calls were even coming in from people who were told about the website from others who'd seen it and planned to rent. Yep! I couldn't believe how smoothly things were running. I was in hog heaven.

It was 2014, Saturday, January 11th when I arrived. Carlos came to pick me up at the airport and drove me to his place where I got my bike. I rarely traveled with a lot of luggage. But believe it or not, with the luggage rack, saddlebags and using bungee cords, you'd be amazed how much stuff you can carry on a bike. Seriously.

After first stopping by the house to drop off my luggage, I ran into town to get groceries. SAM'S and Wally World were just eighteen miles up the road in Lázaro Cárdenas. What's that? Are you laughing? You thought I was out in uncivilized territory. You do know that Wally World is just another name for Walmart, don't you? Anyway, I didn't get too much, knowing I was only going to be there for two weeks.

After settling in that weekend, enjoying the peace and quiet, I decided to take the boat out on Monday. Funny. It was Monday the 13th, not Friday the 13th. But it was the day my life ran off that wonderful straight and smooth highway and onto an unbelievable back road to my Destiny.

My intention was to spend the whole day on the water. With the sun being so bright here in Mexico, I put on a lightweight, long-sleeved shirt, jeans, sneakers and one of my baseball caps. This would help keep me from turning into a 'crispy critter' from sunburn. I considered bringing a jug of Whiskey Sours but just as you don't go drinking and driving on land, you don't go drinking and sailing, either. I had a large jug of water and a picnic basket full of non-perishable goodies. I also brought my fishing equipment, thinking I might catch something to bring home for dinner. It was stashed in the compartment under the back seat. The rod and reel lay on the bottom of the boat.

I also placed my wallet with my passport in a resealable plastic bag and put it in the rear compartment under the back seat of the boat. I didn't want to carry them on me in case I got wet. I always carried them with me in case I was stopped. The Federals and military were constantly patrolling the waters off the coast, probably looking for possible drug situations. Hey. You never know. And I liked to be prepared. Especially, with a boat like mine. I mean, it just looked like it could hold a huge supply of drugs the way it was built.

Unlocking the lock, putting it and the keys in the storage box on top of the post, I pulled off the boat cover, rolled it up and placed it under the front compartment. All the seat cushions were there, too. Up came the anchor. I grabbed the oars, braced myself against the rowing seat and mast and rowed through the light surf out to the very calm sea.

Placing the oars in their respective holders, I raised the sail and slowly headed out. Even though I could usually tell by the position of the sun, I was taking no chances. I always kept a compass in a small box in the compartment under the back seat of the boat. It would also prevent a panic attack if I got out of sight of land. A compass would definitely let me know which way was land. I also kept several squeeze bottles of sunscreen in that compartment to be used by me or any of my guests who might take the boat out. It prevented forgetting to bring some from the house. A lighter and several packs of matches in a plastic bag were also in the small box kept in the compartment in case someone landed on a beach and wanted to build a fire there. Little did I realize but I was going to discover there was another significant item I should have had stashed on the boat. You'll understand what it was as the story progresses. Some of you who are snickering may have already figured out what it was.

The breeze was wonderful and caught the sail. The boat seemed to be moving along at a good clip. Slowly but surely, I headed straight out toward the southwestern horizon. The ocean was calm with only minor swells.

It was early afternoon when suddenly, the wind completely ceased. This was totally surprising to me. There had always been some kind of breeze on the ocean. But now, there wasn't a whisper. I did a quick estimate in my head. With the nice breeze I'd had, I was thinking I'd been traveling maybe three to four miles an hour for the last five hours. This would put me out about some fifteen to twenty miles. Facing toward the mainland in the slight haze, I could only see the mountains I knew were located some five miles inland. This made me realize I was probably out closer to twenty miles. It had been some time since I'd been this far out to sea. It was way too far to row to get back.

It looked like I was going to spend a while in the boat, waiting for the wind to pick up again. I was glad I was smart enough to pack a picnic basket and a jug of water. What is the old Murphy's Law? 'Anything that *can* happen, *will* happen.' So, as the Boy Scouts taught me, 'Be Prepared.'

I did have to laugh. I wasn't totally 'prepared'. I had no flashlight, pillow or a little blanket in the event I had to spend the night. What could I say? But never did I have intentions of being out in the water at night. Guess I learned a big lesson on this trip. I did have the seat cushions, though. They were better than nothing.

Even with the calm rocking of the boat, I wasn't actually able to relax. I did know there were major cargo ships, coming through, heading into and out of the port of Lázaro Cárdenas. I had no desire to get run over by one of them. It was essential I stay a little bit alert.

I was there in the calm for just over an hour when all of a sudden I turned, looking farther out to sea. Something was there that I hadn't noticed before. Maybe four or five miles away. I couldn't believe it. It had to be a mirage. I'd never seen it from shore. But maybe it was too far out to be seen from shore. I shook my head and laughed, "It's a damn island. But how could that be? There are no islands off the southwest coast of Mexico in this area."

Just then, the wind began to pick up. My curiosity got the best of me. I had to go check it out. I could probably be there in about two hours or less. It was going on mid-afternoon and even if I had to spend the night there, I didn't care. I had no plans.

Yep. There it was and it looked to be about a mile and a half wide. I saw the island had the distinctive cone of a volcano. The cone wasn't very high. Actually, it was rather short, seeming to be like maybe the height of two Empire State Buildings with easy-sloping sides. I did understand that this part of the world was seismic because the Ring of Fire came up through this region. But from all the maps I'd ever seen of this area, none showed any island.

I began to giggle, "Maybe I should claim it and sell real estate."

Getting closer to the partially rocky shore, I could see a beautiful sandy beach, leading to a relatively thick jungle beyond. Before I reached the point where the waves began to break, I took down the sail, braced myself and readied the oars for rowing. My timing was great. I caught one wave with the boat and it pushed me through a wide opening among the rocks and nearly to shore. It had to have been around five o'clock when I got there.

I quickly jumped out, grabbed the front of the boat and began pulling it as far toward the beach as I could through the shallow water. Then, I grabbed the anchor and placed it to hold the boat in place. There was no way I was able to pull it up onto the beach. It was way too heavy.

Standing there, I looked up and down the beach. I'm not sure why but suddenly the movie, 'Jurassic Park', popped into my mind. The thought of a T-Rex, bounding down the beach in my direction, was definitely unsettling for a moment. I did snicker nervously. I also realized if there was some kind of danger, all I had to fight it off with was an oar from the boat. I couldn't imagine it being very effective.

My mind began to whirl, trying to think of the kinds of creatures I could expect to see. I know it may sound stupid but I couldn't get the T-Rex out of my head.

Even with the notion of a T-Rex in my head, I knew it was too late to start back to the mainland. I would have to spend the night there. Now, it was time to do a little exploring. I had time. It was late afternoon and it looked like there might be maybe two more hours before sunset. A major question came to my mind. How is it with all the cargo ship traffic through this area, there was no indication of this island on any of the maps I'd seen? I even remembered zooming out when I was using Google Earth on my computer and never recalled seeing an island some twenty-five miles southwest of the mainland. This was very curious.

I peered into the jungle in front of me. Looking to my left and then to my right, I decided to walk to my right, north, up the beach. I started to laugh as I started off… "Heigh Ho!… Heigh Ho!… It's up the beach we go!"

Walking for about fifteen minutes, I couldn't get over what a beautiful beach it was even though there were numerous large outcroppings of volcanic rock. I was also extremely surprised there was no evidence of anyone living there. Very strange. I shook my head. Right after having that thought, I happened to turn to my left, looking into the vegetation. That's when I saw it. A path. Not well defined but obviously a path. Immediately, my stupid imagination went wild. I couldn't get the image from my mind of a T-Rex, coming out of the jungle. "Stop it! Stop it! Stop being such a dumbass! This is the twenty-first century and all dinosaurs have been dead for millions of years. Got it?" And after all, the path was way too narrow to be for a T-Rex. But. Something did make it and I wondered where it went.

Aren't old expressions interesting? It seems there's one suitable for virtually every occasion and circumstance. I looked at the pathway. 'Curiosity killed the cat.' What could I say? I headed to the entrance, crying out, "Meow! Meow!" I shook my head as I laughed.

What a difference in temperature I felt, walking into the jungle. I'm not sure why but I wondered why I didn't hear more sounds. You see all those jungle movies and you'd think the whole zoo was in the vegetation. Not here. There were just the sounds of some distant birds. At least it sounded like it might be birds. That was it. Didn't see a lot of insects, either.

The path looked like it might be used every now and then. Not on a regular basis. Only the tops of the trees were being moved by the breeze. It was virtually still as a mouse at ground level.

The path led me farther and farther into the jungle. Very shortly, I heard the sound of pouring water. Getting closer, I came to a small clearing with a very small waterfall, coming off a ridge about ten feet high and falling into a pool beneath it. A little stream left the pool and disappeared into the jungle to the right.

My curiosity was nagging me again. Where the hell would water come from on an island? Suddenly, I got a little whiff and I could smell a hint of sulfur. My question just got answered. Somehow, the water was percolating up from down in the earth, probably forced up by volcanic heat.

The path led to the left of the waterfall and followed the bottom of a ridge, curving around and deeper into the jungle. In no time at all, the path came to a rough rocky slope. It appeared to be about sixty feet high, not too difficult to climb with a gentle slope, outcroppings and flat areas.

Just then, there came a rumbling sound and the ground began to shake. I stood perfectly still to prevent myself from losing my balance. After a few seconds, it was over. I continued on my quest.

Reaching the top, there was a little open plateau. I turned and could see to the north, east and south. The beach below wasn't visible because of the thick vegetation. There was open ocean in all those directions. I thought I'd be able to see the mainland way to the northeast. It should be some twenty-five or so miles away. But it was a bit hazy. If it had been clearer, I most likely would have at least been able to see the mountains there.

It was also obvious from this vantage point, the island was even larger than I thought. It continued far in a southwesterly direction. The thick jungle directly southwest of the plateau space obscured seeing anything in that direction except for the top of the cone of the volcano in the distance, rising above the greenery. I saw no smoke or steam rising from it. I guess the small quake had no influence on it. Guess all was well. I looked back at the path. Interestingly enough, it led from the plateau and continued into the jungle, westward.

While standing there, I thought of the time and decided that maybe I should get back to the boat, get some water then check out the beach in the other direction. Plus the sun was setting and it would soon start getting dark.

With the light waning, I made a quick walk south down the beach which showed nothing different, just thick jungle to the right just off a wide-open and beautiful beach dotted with many groups of volcanic rock outcroppings. By the time I got back to the boat, it was evening, the sun was below the horizon and I was bushed. Also, the tide had gone out some and now the boat was sitting in much shallower water. There was no way I'd be able to get the boat into deeper water. The thought did cross my mind about what it would be like heading back in the dark. "Probably get run over by a cargo ship."

Sitting in the boat, I started munching on a little snack even though I really wasn't hungry. I was still very confused about the island and why it wasn't on any map. Instantly, my mind went crazy again. It's a secret military base where secret experiments are being done. I yelled out, "Stop it! Stop it! For crying out loud! Geez!"

Again, I realized I was getting a gold star on my 'being prepared'. There were the matches and a lighter in the compartment under the boat's backseat. Just as planned, they'd been put there in case someone wanted to build a little fire on the beach, during an outing. Well, guess what? I ran around quickly, searching for some wood and dead leaves to build a small fire on the beach up from the boat.

But suddenly, I knew I was going to get a black mark. Why?

Remember I mentioned I would realize a very important item I'd neglected to put in the boat? Well, I knew I had to go to the bathroom and had no toilet paper. It was instantly obvious what I had to do. I took off all my clothes, headed just into the jungle and leaned against a tree. That done, I ran out into the surf. That would work. I splashed around a bit after making sure I was cleaned up. I made a mental note to include at least one roll of toilet paper on board in the future. Maybe four. Okay. Yeah. You're laughing again. I hear you.

With the sun now gone, there was nothing to do except try to get comfortable. I grabbed a few cushions from the boat and sat by the fire. As night rolled in, I thought of no reason to sit there, staring into the fire. I really was quite tired. I got dressed, gathered up the seat cushions, placed them in the bottom of the boat under the seats that went from one side of the boat to the other and tried to get some rest. Strangely enough, in no time at all, I was asleep.

Chapter IV

'Bump....... Bump....... Bump.' It was the sound of something hitting up against the boat, waking me up. The tide must have come in and brought a piece of driftwood with it, hitting against the boat.

I'd been lying on my side in the bottom of the boat under the seats near the back end of the boat with my baseball cap covering my face. I wasn't sure what time it was but it seemed to be fairly bright out. Slowly, I worked myself into a sitting position between two seats, facing the rear of the boat. I crawled and looked over the left-hand side of the boat into the water and saw nothing. I then scooted and leaned over the edge to my right and again saw nothing. A questioning expression covered my face.

I shook my head. "What the hell could possibly have made that noise?" I slowly turned, attempting to get up and get out of the boat. Suddenly, I was aware of a man, standing about four feet from the bow of the boat, holding a wooden stick in his right hand. I was so shocked, I almost hurt myself, scrambling toward the back of the boat and falling over one of the seats.

I looked closely at the man. He was tall with long dark brown hair, a scraggly dark brown beard and mustache. The ragged clothes and boots he wore couldn't hide his stocky, muscular build. His chest was covered with thick dark brown hair. That's when I realized, he was wondering who I was. It was written all over his face and in his incredible blue eyes.

I looked directly at him and tried to speak clearly, "Hola. ¿Cómo estás? Mi nombre es Mark." I paused for a moment, hearing no response from the man. I chuckled and commented, "Damn! I know my Spanish is like shit but anyone from Mexico should be able to understand what I just said." I had to admit that he sure did not look like the typical Hispanic man, especially with those blue eyes.

The man looked at me and a huge grin began to fill his face. He started to chuckle then spoke quietly with a voice with the same masculine qualities as Sam Elliott's, "When I saw you sleeping in the boat, I knew you weren't Hispanic. It's now obvious you're from north of the border. But what the hell brought you here? And how did you build the fire?" He looked down at the boat. "Yes, I know you got here in your boat. But what is a guy like you doing down here in Mexico? Well, I'm pretty sure this island is off the coast of Mexico."

I was a bit confused but responded, "I'm down here on vacation."

"Vacation? I'll bet. Must be a son of one of those wealthy, northern industrialists." He snickered.

"Well. Excuse me! I'm not the son of some damn northern

industrialist. I work very hard for a living and I'm down here on vacation. End of story!"

He started to laugh, "Now, don't get your pants in a twist and your bowels in an uproar. I was just surmising."

I shook my head and smiled, "I'm sorry. Sorry for sounding so uppity. And I don't want this to start off on the wrong foot. But you did scare the shit out of me. I had no idea anyone was living on this island. Actually, I didn't even know the damn island existed till yesterday."

He gave a big grin, "Well, the only reason I'm living on this island is because I got marooned here like about eight, maybe nine months ago. I've kinda lost track of time since I fell off the boat. I figured this island was probably just off the coast of Mexico." He put his stick in his left hand, walked over to the boat and extended his right hand toward me. "Sorry. The name's Brody. Brody Hollister. Here! Let me help you up."

I grabbed his hand with both of mine as he pulled me into a standing position. That's when I realized it was obvious he was over six feet tall. "Well. Hello, Brody. Nice to meet you. I'm Mark. Mark Lancaster."

"Yeah. I kinda got that from your Spanish." He began to snicker, "By the way, that's a real nice rig you have there. Isn't it a little wide, though?"

"Thanks. I got it to have fun in and go fishing. Wasn't planning on doing any racing." I changed the subject, "So. Marooned? Fell off a boat? How the hell did that happen? Isn't anybody looking for you? Eight or nine months? Damn! Okay! I know this has got to be one hell of a story. Is there anyone else with you?"

"Nope. I'm here all by my lonesome. There's no sign of anyone else on the island as I've had time to do some exploring. But only around the edges."

"Brody! Is there anything keeping you here? I mean, we can get in my boat here and go back home to the mainland."

Brody shook his head. "There's nothing keeping me here but we can't leave right now."

A questioning expression filled my face. "What? What do you mean we can't leave right now? We can get in my boat and head northeast. The mainland is less than a day's sailing. About seven hours. That way." I pointed to the northeast.

"That's what you think. But are you sure? Not trying to sound all mysterious but there's something weird about this place. Let's head up to camp first. I'll show it to you, so you'll know where it is. Then, we can come back here and I'll try to catch us something for dinner. I'll tell you all about this place. Or at least what I know about it. And you still haven't told me how you lit the fire."

"Let me get my stuff out of the boat first." I grabbed the matches and lighter from under the back seat and held up the plastic bag. "This is how I lit the fire. With the matches."

"Tell me about them as I have never seen anything like them before."

I was rather shocked and surprised that someone had no clue what matches or a lighter were but there had to be some reason. "I will. Later."

Grabbing the picnic basket, I suddenly realized Brody might be hungry. "Brody. Not sure if you might be hungry but I have a few things here in the basket if you want them." I opened the basket and held it in Brody's direction.

Brody walked over and looked into the basket. "Oh, my God! Real food! I haven't had real food since I've been here." He grabbed up one of the bags of chips and looked at it with a questioning expression. After a moment, he pulled on it, popping the bag open. Reaching into the bag he grabbed some chips and started eating them. After a moment, he stopped and looked at me with a questioning expression.

I smiled, "Brody. Eat. Christ. Eat it all. If anyone deserves the damn food you do."

I pulled several cushions from the boat and we sat down on the beach. Brody continued to eat.

"Mark, I swear. I thought I was never going to eat real food again in my life. Thanks."

"Well, I wouldn't go so far as to calling it real food. It's loaded with preservatives and salt. My doctor tells me to stay away from all

this processed stuff. But it does keep really well in these sealed bags."
I grinned, "So, eat up. And here's some water for you to drink. Sorry,
I don't have any sodas with me. And when you're done, I want to
hear all about how the hell you got here."

I held up the ziplock bag containing the lighter and matches.
"Okay. I'll show you these and how they work." I opened the bag
and pulled out one of the packs of matches then set the bag down.
"Here is how matches work." Opening the pack, I pulled one of
the matches from it and then struck the match on the strike pad. I
was making sure Brody could easily see. The match head burst into
flame. I held up the burning match. "And this is how I can light a
fire using matches." I shook the match to put it out. "Now, I will
show you how a lighter works." I put the pack of matches back in the
bag and pulled out the lighter. I held it close to Brody, so he could
see as I flicked the lighter and the flame appeared. "That's how a
lighter works." I let go the lever and the flame went out. I returned
the lighter to the bag and sealed it.

Brody stopped eating and just quietly spoke, "Wow. Those are
amazing."

"Now, you know what matches and a lighter are. You eat the rest
of that stuff and then we can head to your camp."

Brody was hungry. He ate everything left in the basket but it
wasn't that much. When he was finished, I took the empty bags
and placed them in the front storage compartment of the boat, so
they wouldn't litter the beach. I then put the lighter and matches in
the picnic basket with the jug of water. "I have a compass here, too.

No need for it on this island." I turned, looking out to sea. "I don't understand. Seriously. The mainland is right over there." I pointed to the northeast.

"Don't be so sure about that. I'll tell you what I know in a little while. When we get back here later. Here. Let me carry the basket for you." He took the basket out of my hand, grabbed his stick and we headed north, up the beach. "By the way, as we walk along, if you see any pieces of wood, grab it up and bring it. It's not easy keeping the fire going."

Something told me we were going to take the pathway I found the day before. Yep. I was correct as we headed into the jungle. Up the path, past the little waterfall, up the slope to the plateau and then into the jungle on the far side with the path leading in a westerly direction.

I thought about what Brody had said as I grabbed pieces of wood when we saw any. With no matches or lighters, it would be a major chore to keep a fire constantly going. I stopped short and looked at Brody. "Brody! I just realized. If you got marooned somehow, you have nothing."

Brody stopped and looked at me. "Correct. That's one reason why I have to keep the damn fire burning if I want to try and cook anything. That's also why I wanted to know how you started one."

"Well. Now, that I have the matches and a lighter, you won't have to worry about keeping it going continuously. They are just some of the things I usually keep in the little compartment under the back seat of the boat. My fishing gear is there, too. The rod and reel are in the bottom of the boat near the back."

A big smile covered his face and his blue eyes seemed to sparkle, "Well, I'll be damned. Fishing gear, too. Yep. This must be my lucky day, finding you on the beach."

Soon, we came out to a large plateau valley area with high bluffs on the northern and southern sides. At the far southwest end of the valley was more jungle. In the far southwest corner, it began to slope down again. I could see the top of the volcanic cone in the distance directly to the southwest. On the northern side of the valley was a fairly large lake, going right up against the northeastern bluffs. We headed to the northeast edge of the lake.

"Camp is near the lake and at the base of the bluffs there." Brody pointed with his stick.

Arriving at his little camp, I saw he had a fairly large piece of canvas over some crudely constructed supports. Off to the side was a rock construction. It soon became evident. It was where Brody had his fire. We piled the pieces of wood we'd found by the rock construction.

Brody looked around. "Well, now you know where camp is located."

I looked under the canvas and saw a pile of palm leaves. I assumed it was Brody's bed. Suddenly, it became quite clear to me how difficult it would be to be placed somewhere and not have anything. You'd have to make do with what you could find. I shook my head. "This has been a real bitch for you, I'm sure. I'm surprised you've been able to make it."

"You're right there. Funny how you quickly learn what's important." He gave a reluctant nod.

"Okay. As I mentioned, since I have fishing gear in the boat, maybe it might be a good idea to get back to the beach and try to catch something to eat." Looking around, I saw several shells. Some were small and a few were large. There was also a very large shell from a turtle by the fire pit. Probably from finds among the rock outcroppings and sand along the beach. I then realized that Brody may have caught it and eaten it. Suddenly, I remembered. "I can't believe it but I also have a knife, fork and spoon in the basket. I have a feeling they'll come in very handy."

Brody clapped his hands. "I'll bring my spear stick in case I see something around the rocks."

On the way back to the beach, I wanted to get myself familiar with where I was. Brody was leading the way and we didn't get a chance to do any major talking. I wasn't concerned as I knew this would take place when we were less occupied with other things.

When we arrived back on the beach, he led me to a large group of volcanic rock outcroppings, sticking out of the ocean and the beach. "I've had pretty good luck over here." He pointed.

"Don't forget. We can go out in the boat as well if you like." I could see the boat not far down the beach.

"How about tomorrow? I'd love to get out in that rig of yours. Maybe one day we can sail around the island and I can show you a few things."

"One day? I thought we could get in the boat tomorrow and head home. You're making it sound like we're going to be here for a while. Why is that?"

"There's not been a quake. The last one late yesterday afternoon closed the hole." He spoke so matter of fact.

"Quake? Hole?" A questioning expression filled my face.

He pointed straight out from the shore. He was pointing to the northeast and the mainland. "Out there. There's a hole. It took me some time to realize it was there but it is. It's closed right now. The quakes somehow open and close it. When it's open, sometimes stuff comes through it, drifting in from the outside world. That's why I was on the beach this morning. As I said, the second quake happened late yesterday afternoon and closed the hole. I was coming to see if anything had drifted in. I'd have come sooner but I was tired. The first quake happened in the early afternoon. Yesterday. But I'd gone to get wood to bring back to camp. That took all day. I knew there wasn't any rush because whatever the ocean brought in would be here today. And so it was. You."

I laughed, "You've got to be kidding me."

"Nope. I finally realized this is how I must have gotten here."

I turned and headed to the boat. "Let me go get the fishing gear from the boat. Be back in a few." I got what I needed and quickly returned.

We headed out onto the rocks. Brody started looking down into the adjacent waters.

I climbed out to one of the nearby rocks and got my fishing rod ready. With a quick jerk of the rod, the lure landed some twenty feet out from the rocks. The bob float was holding the lure and hook below the surface. I sat down on the rock and waited. "Okay. I'm ready. 'Enquiring minds want to know.' I want to hear your story. I didn't ask sooner because I wanted you to do it while we were not involved with doing something else. I wanted it to be while we were sitting down and comfortable."

Brody responded, "If you must know, I'm here all because of gold. If it weren't for my desire to try and strike it rich, I wouldn't be here. Yep. All because of gold."

Chapter V

I turned my head toward Brody. "What? Gold? I must admit, that would've been the last reason why I'd have thought you wound up here. Sorry for interrupting. Keep going."

Brody continued, "Everyone heard about the gold and how many were becoming wealthy overnight. I'm not sure if the stories were overblown or not but I wanted to try my luck. I wasn't the only one. There was a slew of us who left everything behind in Virginia and the Carolinas in the care of others, so we could go find gold. We took a boat down and finally got to Panama. It's funny how many got seasick on the trip." He shook his head. "Just not accustomed to the pitch and roll on the water. You know, I think everyone was glad when we finally got to stand on dry land again."

"Brody. Sorry to interrupt again but I didn't know there was gold in Panama. And what the hell are you doing out here? This is way up the coast from Panama."

"Don't rush me. Don't rush me. You'll know in a minute." He paused briefly to poke his spear stick at a fish. "Damn. Missed." He gave a grunt of dissatisfaction, "We wanted to get to Panama because from where we landed, that's where it's the shortest distance to the west coast, so we could get another ship heading up the coast. After everyone got their stomachs back again, we all got a ship on the west coast to head north. On the way up the coast, we hit a storm. It was night time and the winds were horrific. Several of us were getting sick and went up on deck to puke over the side."

"That's when it happened. The top section of one of the masts broke before they could lower the topsail and it went over the side into the water. Guys were grabbing anything to cut the ropes to prevent more damage. Unfortunately for me, the railing on which I was leaning got hit by the falling mast section and over I went. Right into the drink. One of the sailors threw me two life belts in hopes they might possibly save me."

"There was no way they could stop and look for me with all they were trying to do to keep the ship from faltering. I knew I was a goner when I saw the ship, heading away from me. It wasn't easy fighting the waves and wind that night. It seemed like the night lasted forever. But as the early rays of the sun began to come up over the eastern horizon, the storm stopped."

"That's when I saw the island out on the western horizon. I knew if I was going to live, I had to get to it. And so, I started making my way to come here. It took almost all day but I finally got up on the beach and was exhausted. I'm not sure how long I lay there but I knew I had to get out of the sun before I got burned. I crawled up to the jungle and got into some shade. I fell asleep."

"I was awakened by a violent shaking. As quickly as it began, it was over. It was just after sunset. I slept right there till morning. When I woke up, I looked out at the beach. That's when I saw the top section of the mast, drifting in the surf. I used as much of it as I could. The canvas covering back at camp. That's the sail. I also saved all the rope from the rigging. I was never sure when it might come in handy."

"It wasn't easy in the beginning. I had to find fruit trees and stuff to eat. I found several trees with fruit on them and some vines, too. Not sure what they are but I saw the birds and bugs eating them, so I was pretty sure I could eat them. When you're hungry, you eat what you can find."

I raised my hand. "Question. Back to the gold. If the gold wasn't in Panama, where the hell was it if you were sailing up the west coast?"

"Why, California! Of course! Everyone knows that!" He looked at me like I was an idiot.

"Wait a minute. Wait a minute! What the hell are you talking about? Gold? California?" I gave Brody a weird look.

Brody looked right at me. "Yes! Of course! California! Have you been living under a rock? A great number of folks are trying to get there to look for it. Many are going overland from the east coast but I heard some bad stories about how difficult and dangerous it was to make the trip. So, I decided to take the route by sea. It was longer but I thought a lot safer. Guess I was wrong. Instead of being killed by

bandits or indians, I get marooned on an island. Ain't that ironic?"
He shook his head and laughed.

I stood up and put my hands on my hips, still holding the fishing
rod in my left hand. I yelled out, "No! No! No! Wait! Wait! Wait
a minute!!! California for gold. Killed by bandits or indians? This
is ridiculous. For Christ's sake, it sounds like you're talking about
the California gold boom of the early eighteen fifties. Okay. Okay.
What's the joke?" I looked right at him.

Brody twisted his head to the side. "Of course, I am. Then,
you do know of it. They discovered gold there at Sutter's Mill and
everyone wants to get some of it."

"BRODY!" I yelled, "But that discovery was in eighteen
forty-eight!"

"That's right. It's eighteen forty-nine. No. By now, it's probably
eighteen fifty." He stared right at me.

Suddenly, the wheels started turning in my head. I could see
from his expression he was dead serious and not lying. "Holy shit!"
I was speechless for the longest time. I was so shocked, I sat down
again on the rock. Finally, I gained my senses and spoke, "Holy shit!
Holy shit! Holy shit! Oh, my God!" My mind began to analyze what
Brody had said. The ship he was on had masts and sails. The gold
rush in California was in the early 1850s. The people going out there
were called 'Forty-Niners'. Suddenly, it became perfectly clear. For
Brody, it was 1850. For me, it was 2014.

I looked right at Brody. "Oh. My. God. Brody. This is weird as shit. Somehow for you, it's eighteen fifty. But for me..." I paused, "I know this is going to sound so off-the-wall for you. But. For me, it's... it is two thousand and fourteen. Over one hundred and fifty years from eighteen fifty."

Brody gave a strange expression. And spoke quietly, "What!? Two thousand fourteen!?" He paused for a moment, "But. But that can't be. No! You're kidding me! Tell me you're kidding me. No!" He paused again and shook his head, "Seriously? Mark. You ARE pulling my leg? What?"

"Ah. Nope. For me, it's two thousand and fourteen." I reached up and scratched my beard. "Do me a favor. Run over to the boat and check in the back compartment. You'll find a clear plastic bag there with my wallet in it."

He looked at me strangely. "A plastic bag?"

I shook my head. "You'll know it when you see it. It's sort of like the bags of chips and stuff you ate earlier. Yep! Like the one, I have the lighter and matches in. I'll explain later." It now made total sense as to why he had no idea what matches and a lighter were.

Brody quickly did as I asked and was back in only a few minutes, holding the bag in the air and a questioning expression on his face. He walked over and sat on a nearby rock.

"That's it. Now. Open the bag. You have to pull the zippy top apart to open it."

Brody grabbed the two top flaps and pulled. The bag opened.

"This thing's made of plastic? I've never seen anything like it before. It's like flexible glass. So, those bags of chips and food were in the same kind of bags?"

"Yes. Plastic. I'll tell you about it another time. Now, check the things in my wallet."

Brody opened the wallet and saw the passport tucked in the left side. He opened the passport to the page with my picture and information. He started to chuckle, "The picture of you has color. Wow. It says you were born in…" He paused, looked at me strangely then back at the passport again. "In nineteen seventy-four. In June. It was issued in two thousand and eleven and will expire in two thousand and twenty-one."

"Yeah. I'll be the big Four-O in June. Okay. Keep looking."

Brody pulled out my Discover card. "What is Discover? And it's made of a strange material."

"It's plastic money. I'll explain it to you sometime, too. And it's made of plastic just like the bag but a harder kind."

He then pulled out my driver's license. "The picture on this thing has color, too. And it's made of…" He looked at me. "Plastic?"

I nodded. "You've got it. That's right."

"It says 'driver license'. For what?"

"We have to have those if we want to drive cars and trucks.

I'll tell you all about those another time as well. Brody. Much has happened since your time."

Brody put everything back in the wallet, into the plastic bag and resealed it. He spoke quietly, "Oh, my God. That hole isn't only a way to another world but to another time, too. Holy cow. Geez. I kinda wish I had a drink right now."

I nodded. "That makes two of us."

At that, something tugged at my line. After a little effort, I'd caught a decent-sized fish. I hauled it in, held it up and smiled, "We have dinner!"

"Okay. Let's get it to camp and on the fire." Brody clapped his hands. "Now, much makes sense to me. Your clothes, the stuff you have in the basket. Thought at first, it was stuff only rich folks could afford. But now, I have a million questions. You bet I do."

"I'm sure you do but let's stop by the boat again, so I can get some sunscreen. It'll help us from getting sunburned." That's when I remembered Brody's comment about me being the son of a wealthy northern industrialist. Yes. It was beginning to all fall into place. All except how to get home again. Would it still be possible? I knew Brody had much more to say about the hole. I needed to find out as much about it as possible.

We didn't do much talking on the way back to camp but we did pick up a few more pieces of wood for the fire. Brody commented as he picked one piece up, "There's a very large area on the south side of the island where there must've been some sort of heat or gas flow from the volcano and it killed all the trees. I get a lot of wood from there since it's all in one place." He grinned, "I call it my woodpile."

Back at camp, Brody stirred the coals in the fire pit and placed a few new pieces of wood on it. Soon, there was a nice small fire. In the meantime, I took the knife from the picnic basket and did what I could with the fish to get the scales off and guts out of it. When I was finished, Brody took it and rinsed it off in the nearby lake to make sure all the scales were gone.

Brody took a piece of vine and wrapped it around the fish several times then to a stick and dangled it above the fire to cook. "First few times I did this, the damn fish fell in the fire and I had to get a stick and get it out. Found out you have to be really careful how close you get it to the flames or you can lose it."

I sat there watching. "I'm still amazed you survived for so long with nothing. Damn. No fishing gear, no pots and pans, no grill top, no knife, no nothing. Geez."

"You've got that right. I use those bigger shells over there as plates. Another one has a fairly sharp edge. I use it to cut up stuff and scale fish." He shook his head. "I found the big turtle shell on the beach and use it to carry stuff. Especially, when I go for wood. I've attached some rope to it from the mast rigging, so I can drag it along. It's also how I got the fire here." He paused and stared out into space, "I'll tell you about that sometime. That was one hell of a day. Do you know how hot lava is?"

Soon, the fish was done. Brody also had a few pieces of fruit he'd picked from the jungle. I saw they were guava and papaya. Birds must have eaten the fruit on the mainland and carried the seeds here. I was curious if there were any other edibles that the seeds were brought by birds. We sat and ate. I gave Brody the fork and I used the spoon.

Afterward, Brody suggested we head down to the beach, so he could explain about the hole. He said to carry the shells, knife, spoon, fork and cooking stick with us to wash later in the hot springs. They were located on the plateau above where the little waterfall was. Water, running from the springs, fed the waterfall.

When we came out of the jungle, we turned south and walked to the boat. We both sat on the back end and looked out to sea. Brody pointed toward the northeast horizon. "The hole is probably about two maybe three miles out. Just a guess. Never knew it was there until the day I was on the beach. As you see, you can't see it now. It's invisible. I'd been walking along the beach, looking for a place to maybe spear a fish when a quake hit. It almost knocked me down. But it didn't last long."

"I was looking out to sea when suddenly, I noticed a strangeness, covering a very large area out there. Kind of like a large irregular arch with a base about two miles wide and in the middle maybe a quarter of its width in height. The entire image in that area just shimmered for some thirty or forty seconds and then was clear again. I had to look closely. That's when I realized the area inside the arch was slightly different from the surrounding area. I sat on the beach and watched it even more carefully. When I tried to match up the cloud formations, they didn't. It was an incredible realization."

"I watched for a while but then knew I had to go find something to eat or I was going to starve for the day. Funny how much our stomachs rule our lives." He snickered, "I went back to where I was trying to make a camp. I picked there because of the lake. I can drink the water."

"For two days in a row, I came to this spot and looked out. After examination, I could see the hole was still there. During that time period, several things came floating in. That wooden barrel I have up at camp. Several odds-and-ends things."

"And that's when there was another small quake. It happened during the night. The next day I came down and I could see the hole was gone. It was invisible again. Starting to put two and two together, I theorized the hole and the quakes were connected."

"Now, you should have seen the time a quake happened early in the morning. I guess it was like in a month or a little more of me being here. I quickly got up and ran down here. The hole was already open and you should have seen it. The whole area of the arch was dark. There was a huge and violent storm on the other side. I could see the lightning and hear the thunder. It almost was funny. Like looking through a giant window. Everything here was calm as calm could be. But from the hole, the rough waves poured over into this side. But the sky in this place and around the arch was a clear sunny day. Yep. It was something to see."

"I watched it not sure for how long. Finally, the storm there eased and began to diminish. Again, while the hole remained open, stuff would float in from the other side. I never knew what would come in. That's why I'd always come check the beach after the second quake. Have to tell you. I was totally shocked when this last one hit and come to find this boat and you here in it."

I had a question, "How often do these quakes happen?"

"You never know. And the time between while the hole is open has no set time, either. Sometimes it's for a couple of days and sometimes it's just for a couple of hours. They do get the hot springs jumping, though. While I've been here, there have been maybe fifteen to twenty times."

"If you've been here for eight or nine months and for you, it's eighteen fifty and now, I'm here and it's January two thousand and fourteen, it's obvious the hole is definitely not in sync with time. It's not just a hole but a portal in time." As I sat there, finally understanding what had happened, I realized why I never saw the arch before coming to the island. I was too close to it to know it was there. The reason I didn't see it later when I was on the plateau, is because the quake had happened before I got there and closed the portal.

"Damn. Guess I'll have to stop calling it the hole. You're right. It's really a time portal. Wow."

"Yes. When it opens, there's no telling where you would be in time if you went back through it. There are no guarantees you'd return to your own time. This is something we need to talk about because if we ever decide to take our chances and go back through the portal, there is no telling where we would end up in the past. That's totally not cool."

"Cool?" Brody looked at me strangely.

"Oh. Cool. It's a term from the nineteen sixties and means terrific, great, really good. It's slang. Like 'hip' or 'groovy'. They have a similar meaning." After a slight pause, I continued, "So. It's also obvious you have no idea what's beyond this horizon on the mainland or even if there is a mainland. Maybe we should check it out sometime."

Brody looked at me and nodded. "Yes, I guess we could. I agree, now that I understand the possible consequences of sailing back through the portal. I don't think there would be any problem checking out the mainland. If we sail over to it and not go through the portal, we would still be in the same time period as the island."

"You are correct. Everything we see and every place we can reach from here is in the time period of the island since we would not be going through the portal." Then, I suddenly imagined a land of dinosaurs just over the horizon. The thought made me start laughing nervously.

"What's so funny?" Brody didn't understand.

"It's my crazy mind. I could imagine us sailing out and over to the mainland and run into a T-Rex. Not pretty." I started laughing nervously again.

"A T-Rex?"

"Yes. You know. A giant dinosaur." I laughed again and let out a loud roar.

Brody shook his head. "Giant dinosaur?"

"Yeah. Godzilla! Maybe Rodan!!" I laughed really loud. "No. Not Godzilla or Rodan." But then, I suddenly stopped. I stared right at Brody. I spoke quietly, "But of course, you don't know. The word 'dinosaur' didn't even get coined until less than a decade before you left to go to California. If I remember correctly, major finds of dinosaur remains weren't discovered until the mid to late eighteen hundreds. You have no idea what the hell I'm talking about. Damn!"

I stood up, pulled my elbows against my stomach and walked, rocking back and forth, making loud annoying sounds. I turned to Brody. "Now, think of me as a big huge lizard twelve feet tall. You do know what a lizard is, don't you? Godzilla was two hundred feet tall at least but he was fake. Only in the movies." I continued to walk and roar.

Brody started laughing, "You can't be serious. You ARE joking, aren't you? What are movies?"

I stopped and put my hands on my hips. "No. I'm not. They were huge creatures and they lived like over sixty-five million years ago. They got wiped out by a monster asteroid hitting the earth. Long story. I'll have to tell you all about them sometime. Over the decades, many skeletons have been found and are in museums all over the world. I'll also tell you about movies another time. So much has happened since the mid-eighteen hundreds."

"Okay. But it really does sound a bit fishy to me." Brody grinned, "And you say sixty-five million years ago. But I have been told the earth is only six thousand years old."

I cried out, "WRONG! And you probably heard that shit in church, didn't you? Well, let me tell you. THAT is total bullshit. The earth is millions of years old, not six thousand. We'll talk about THAT sometime down the road, too."

Brody chuckled, "From your reaction, I can't wait for THAT discussion." He flexed his eyebrows several times.

I turned, looking up and down the beach. "You're going to have to show me your island. Let me know where things are and I can help you get things and hopefully, it'll make it easier for you, too. If we can't get off this rock until there's another quake, we need to make the best of it."

"Sounds good to me. How about we get in your boat and travel around the island tomorrow? I think it'll be quicker than walking. Took me over eight days to do it. And those were very long days."

"And since we have a lighter and fishing gear, we can fish from the boat and cook it on a fire on the beach. I have a feeling it's going to take at least two days, maybe three, to sail around it if it took you eight to walk it." I shook my head. "Are there any interesting things I should see?"

"Not real sure. I've only explored around where the camp is located and near the beaches. Not had a chance to get to the interior. Now, let's head to the hot springs. We'll wash the things we brought.

One pool is cool enough to get in it. I go there and take my bath and get my clothes as clean as I can."

"Is it far from here? I sure could use a good bath right now."

"Nope. Come on. It's above the waterfall. I'll show you." Brody stood up. "Follow me."

We headed into the jungle and to the little waterfall. We went to the left of the waterfall then up and around to the right on top of the area above the waterfall. After about fifteen minutes, we came to a place with several hot springs, forming small ponds. A few had thick steam, rising from them. The smell of sulfur was in the air.

Brody pointed at the ones that were steaming. "Those are way too hot to get in. I thought about cooking food in them but the taste of sulfur got into the food, so I knew it wasn't the way." He then pointed to a smaller pool where the water from the hotter pools was draining. After placing the items we brought in one of the really hot springs, he took off all his ragged clothes and boots. He placed his boots on a nearby rock, laid his clothes in the water of another of the hotter pools then walked over, got into the smaller pool and sat down. He looked at me. "Come on in. The water's fine. And remember. No peeing in the water."

We both laughed as I took off my clothes and sneakers and set them with Brody's boots. They weren't dirty enough yet to put in the hot water. I slowly walked into the pool and sat down.

Brody began to splash and lay down in the water and use his hands to scrub over his furry body, hair and furry face which had some nine months of growth. I followed suit and was surprised how refreshing it was. "This is really nice. A little smelly but the warm water feels great."

We stayed in the water some thirty minutes then got out. Brody took a stick and pulled his clothes from the spring and placed them on a nearby rock, so they could cool and drain. I was still wet but put on my shirt, pants and sneakers. Brody put on his boots. We pulled the cooking stick, shells, knife, fork and spoon out of the spring and let them cool on a rock. Finally, we gathered everything up and headed back to camp. We first stopped by the boat and hung Brody's wet clothes on nearby bushes to dry.

I had to smile, seeing Brody walking along in only his boots. He was such a handsome man. I was trying to think of a way to trim his hair, beard and stache for him. I was sure it would be less of a bother for him and I just knew it would make him much more handsome.

When we reached the camp, I spoke up, "Since there's a bunch of cushions in the boat, why don't we sleep there tonight? It might be a little bit more comfortable. The seats are high enough that we can lay under them and rest."

Brody agreed, "That would be great. I have to tell you. This pile of palm leaves isn't the best mattress."

"We can come back here in the morning and get whatever you think would be good to have with us sailing around the island."

Brody called out, "That sounds good."

"Cool!" I shouted.

Brody looked at me with a weird expression that quickly turned into a huge smile. He yelled, "Cool!"

We both roared with laughter.

On the walk back to the boat, I started thinking about the portal. "Brody, you do know that we could get in the boat the next time there is a quake. When the portal opens, we could sail right through it and leave the island. BUT! Here is the issue. Since the portal opens to different time periods in the past, we would not know to what time we were headed into. And once through the portal and it closed, we would most likely be forever stuck wherever we were. Doing this will be a major, major decision and discussion that we need to have. We both must agree on doing it. The consequences could be disastrous."

"I see what you mean. You are correct and I agree. We really do need to talk about it. Once we do it, there would be no turning back."

Because of the uncertainty of what we could run into by going through the portal, it made making that decision very scary. Right now we were safe and in a place that was tolerable for the time being. I was at least glad of that.

Chapter VI

It was day three for me on the island. I say day three but in reality, it is really day two and a quarter since I didn't actually arrive until very late afternoon on that first day. When I woke up, Brody's arm was around me and his chest up against my back. It had been some time since I'd had a man this close to me, especially one wearing no clothes. I was rather surprised. Especially, with someone with nineteenth century thinking. Of course, there were gay guys back then but the whole 'gay thing' in that time period was very, very closeted. But, hey! I wasn't complaining, being next to a handsome man like Brody.

Suddenly, Brody woke. He quickly removed his arm and pulled away. He spoke softly, "Sorry. Didn't mean to get so close. Sorry. Sorry."

I rolled over and looked at him. "Brody. Hey. Not to worry. Did you hear any complaints?"

"Well, most guys in my time period would've probably punched me out." He spoke rather gruffly.

I grinned, "Most guys in my time period would probably have punched you out, too. But I'm different. I thought it was nice. I liked it."

He gave me a weird look, "No. No way. What are the chances? But."

"If you're wondering what I think you're thinking, you're correct. And I'll tell you. The whole issue in two thousand fourteen is a hell of a lot more open than it was in eighteen fifty. It's a lot more accepted now than in your time. Not totally as there are still ignorant assholes who refuse to accept the legitimate facts on the subject. But a vast majority have no problem with it."

"Wow. Really? Things must've come a very long way. Men like me have to be so careful. We have to play this stupid silly game."

"Of that, I'm sure. In my time, things have changed. Yes, they have. But not without major confrontations. It also took information coming from the medical fields on the subject, indicating it is not a choice. We are born this way. There's still a long way to go. But we don't have to hide who we are anymore unless you work for some ignorant company or some intolerant religious organization. Believe it or not, it may even happen that marriage between two men or two women will be legalized not too far down the road."

"Holy shit! Really?" He sat up. "Are you serious?"

"As a heart attack." I sat up. "So, not to worry about you lying with me like that. It was nice. And whether you know it or not, you're very easy on the eyes."

Brody bent his head down. "You really think I look good?"

"Look good? You're a very handsome and sexy man. If you were to trim all that hair and fur on your face, put on some decent clothes and walk into any bar, you'd have to beat the guys off of you."

"Bars? You mean like saloons?"

"Yep. Saloons are now called 'bars'. And ones for men like me are called 'gay bars'. They're legal. The term 'gay' has been used for some time now. I think it's because it's easier than saying 'homosexual' all the time." I saw the questioning look on Brody's face. It made me snicker, "Sorry. I forgot that you would never have heard the word 'homosexual' as it had not come into the vocabulary until later in the eighteen hundreds."

"Oh, my God. That's absolutely amazing. You're going to have to tell me more about it."

"I will. But I think we need to go get your clothes, so you can put them on. We will then head to the camp and get the stuff we want to take with us on our little trip around the island. I'll put stuff in the picnic basket. You might even bring the turtle shell. You never know. We might see something where that shell could come in handy. I try to be prepared for whatever might come along."

Brody got dressed and we hurriedly went back to the campsite and got what we needed. Brody grabbed his length of rope. He said it was about twenty feet long, "You never know when things like this might come in handy." He put his left arm through the loops, over his head and onto his right shoulder.

Returning to the boat, we put everything in it and put the anchor up in the front. Since the tide was in again, we both started pushing it into the surf. Once it was clear of the sandy bottom, we turned it, facing out to sea and jumped in. Brody sat on the rowing seat and took the oars. With strong rowing action, he had us out to clear water in no time and up went the sail. Brody put the oars back in their racks. I sat in the back and used the rudder to steer. We headed to go around the southwest side of the island.

It soon became evident that the island was long and narrow, situated in a northeast-southwest direction and perpendicular to the mainland. The volcano was on the southwest end of the island.

The wind was very good and we were moving through the water quite well. We were out far enough, so not to hit any rocks. The beaches were beautiful with the thick jungle beyond. I could see several areas along the beach where the sand areas were completely interrupted by areas of lava rock formations, extending up into the jungle. No wonder it took Brody the time it did to walk around the island on the beaches. Climbing over or around these formations wouldn't have been easy.

After about twenty minutes, Brody mentioned we were coming up to the place he called the woodpile. And there it was. A wide swath of trees, completely dead, from the beach all the way up toward the volcano. There must have been some pyroclastic flow or hot gas flow, devastating everything in its path.

"Maybe we should stop and get some wood? It'll make it so we won't have to look for any later on." I suggested.

"Great idea. Head through those rock formations there." He pointed to a wide opening in the volcanic outcroppings.

Collecting wood, several times he threw the rope over a limb and we both pulled to bring it down. Hitting the ground, it broke into many pieces. Brody would take some of them and hit them on a rock to break them into smaller lengths. We gathered up a huge amount of wood since there was plenty of room in the boat before heading out again.

While we were there, Brody showed me the path that went up the hill to the right and east, eventually to the plateau and the lake containing fresh water. This is the path he'd always taken to come for wood. It was much easier than coming by way of the beach.

After collecting a good amount of wood, it was time to travel onward. The sun was high in the sky when we continued on our way.

Shortly, I noticed whiffs of steam coming from a place where the rocks met the water. "What is that?" I pointed.

Brody looked to where I was pointing. "It's where I used to get my fire if mine went out. It's very hot there."

It was quite obvious. A small flow of lava was slowly oozing into the water there. The island was still growing.

After a while, Brody called out, "How about I do a little fishing while we move along?"

"Great idea. If you catch more than one, we can put water in the turtle shell and keep them there. Here. Dump everything out of the picnic basket. It has no holes in it. You can scoop water up with it if we need to. Maybe keep the fish in it if they're not too big."

After a little while, I began to question, "I noticed I've not seen nor heard any animals. Are there any?"

"In the time I've been here, I haven't seen any. I guess there's no way for them to get on the island. Now, there are lots of birds but that's about it. I've searched for some of the birds to see if I could get some eggs to eat but so far haven't had any luck with that."

"In any of your exploring, did you see any evidence of others who may have stumbled on the island and got caught here?"

"So far, nothing. But remember. I haven't done much exploring, especially in the island's interior. I just haven't had time."

"Yep. I totally get it. Maybe with me here, it'll be easier to do the necessary things and have some time left over to check things out."

Brody nodded. "I thought the same thing."

For a moment, I realized that no one on the mainland knew of my absence. Living alone, no one would wonder until some major time had passed. But I couldn't worry about that now. What was happening here on the island was the situation at hand.

By late afternoon, we decided to go ashore and set things up for the night. Brody had caught two smaller fish and he'd placed them in the basket. We were finally down on the southwestern side of the island. I directed the boat toward the beach and Brody lowered the sail. He took over and rowed us through the surf and right up near the beach. I got out and placed the anchor down.

Brody grabbed the basket and brought it up to the beach. "How does this spot look for building our fire?"

"Great. I'll bring some wood and the lighter." I started gathering several small pieces of wood from the boat.

"I'll go see about getting some dry leaves to get the fire started. Don't start the fire yet. I want to watch you use the lighter." Brody jogged off toward the edges of the jungle. In no time at all, he returned with a huge hand full of dry material. He placed it on the ground. "I'll get the fish ready." He took the knife and basket with the two fish, went to a rock near the edge of the surf and went to work. "When I get this done, maybe we can check out the jungle a bit and see if there are any fruit trees around. Hell. You never know."

Brody finished with the fish and it was time to start the fire. He was quite impressed at the lighter. He also realized it was made of plastic as well.

With the fire started and the fish ready for cooking, we decided to check out the local jungle. Brody had put fresh seawater in the basket and put the cleaned fish in it. He put the lid on it, so the birds wouldn't think it was for them.

Brody had his walking stick with him and it was a good thing. It wasn't easy making way through some of the vines and stuff. I dragged the turtle shell to carry anything we found. Eventually, we got into the jungle and it wasn't as congested with vegetation as near the beach. We walked in for what seemed maybe twenty minutes. We came upon a number of guava and papaya trees on the edge of a small clearing. There was a good reason for the clearing. A lot of rock was near the surface. Nothing could grow there.

Across the clearing was the side of a cliff. It was obviously part of the base of the volcano. It was covered with vines and foliage. I realized the vines had passion fruit on them. "Wow. There's passion fruit over there on the vines." I was glad to see that. It was something else we could add to our diet. I remembered information from documentaries I had seen on volcanos, indicating how the soil around them was excellent for growing things.

I looked up, facing toward the sloping cone. Suddenly, all those Jules Verne novels popped into my mind. I looked at Brody. "I was just thinking about some of the old novels I've read about mysterious islands and lost lands. They all were interesting adventures."

"I hope they had happy endings." He chuckled. He looked at one of the fruit trees. "Okay. I'm going to climb up one and knock down some fruit."

"Sounds good. I'll try and catch them and put them in the turtle shell."

I turned to see Brody hitting at a group of papayas. Shortly, a few came falling down. I yelled out, "Good job. Now, don't fall and break your ass." I did catch a few but the rest fell to the ground. He hit at a few more, knocking them down. "I think that'll do us for a while." He started down the tree.

I ran over and pulled a few guavas off a nearby tree. "I got us a few guavas. I think they're ripe enough to eat. I put them in the turtle shell." I ran over to the vines, pulled some of the passion fruit off and brought them to the turtle shell.

"We'll have to remember about the passion fruit here. I've not seen any around the valley back at the lake. Think it's time to head back to the boat." Brody pulled a few vines as we headed back to the beach, so he could wrap the fish.

After eating and drinking from the jug of water we sat by the fire to talk.

"Mark, there are so many questions I want to ask. All that's happened in the years from my time to yours. I can only imagine. You'll probably say they flew to the moon." He laughed and slapped his leg.

"Well, Brody. They have. Several times."

Brody was shocked, "No way. You're shitting me?"

"Nope. Back in the late sixties. The nineteen sixties."

"Oh. Wow! Geez. Are there people there?"

I shook my head. "No. No people. There's no atmosphere for them to breathe. Sorry. They did put up a flag there."

"Speaking of flags. I noticed one on your hat. And a picture of a man. Is that some club or special group?"

"Oh, no. It's about a very horrible time in American history. Well, history for me. It hasn't happened yet for you. In eighteen sixty-one, the Civil War broke out between the southern and northern states. The man pictured on my hat is Robert E. Lee. He was from Virginia and led the Southern Confederate forces. It was terrible. Many in the South lost everything. It lasted a few years and it was over when Lee surrendered. The flag on my hat was the battle flag carried by the southern troops."

"You mean folks who lived in Virginia lost what they had?"

"In most cases, yes."

"Then, what I left behind there is gone?"

"Most likely. Plantations were looted and burned. Richmond was burned to the ground. So was Atlanta."

Brody looked at me with sad eyes, "I have nothing left to go back to. All those years of work. Gone."

"Brody. I'm so sorry. My family was from Virginia and we lost the plantation and everything, too. It was near Richmond. But actually, it was a good thing. It began the movement to free all the people in slavery. Finally, it was understood that ALL MEN were created equal and that included all those who had been in slavery. Believe it or not, it took a protest movement in the early nineteen sixties to try and eliminate laws and rulings that continued putting folks of color in second-class citizenry. It was called the Civil Rights Movement. We'll have to talk about it one of these days."

Brody tipped his head to the side with a questioning look on his face, "Really? I used to deal with a lot of folks who had farms and plantations around Richmond. Yeah. I had a good-sized store in Richmond. Sold building supplies, farm equipment and stuff like that."

I chuckled, "I wonder if any of my relatives bought stuff from you. The plantation was south and west of the James River."

He smiled and began to snicker, "The only major plantation that is south and just west of the James is Whitby. They are wonderful folks." He paused for a moment and then gasped and yelled, "They are the Lancasters!! No way!!"

To say, I was shocked would be putting it mildly. I started to laugh, "Yep. Those are the ones."

Brody looked at me with shock and surprise written all over his face, "You have to be kidding me. You have to be kidding me! Whitby Plantation!!?" And those Lancasters are your relatives!?"

"You got it. Whitby Plantation belonged to my ancestors! I can't believe it but you knew my relatives from that time."

Brody called out loud, "You're shitting me!? This is unreal! What are the chances!?"

"Yep. But it's all gone now."

Brody finally gathered his senses. "Well, I'll be blessed. This is bizarre as all get out." Brody looked square at me. "Now, what the hell are the chances of me, being from the mid-eighteen hundreds, knowing family members of yours and you are from two thousand and fourteen?"

I shook my head. "You're telling me? Sometime you're going to have to tell me about my ancient relatives."

Brody smiled, "Well, as you would say it, they are really cool folks."

We both laughed.

"Since that time, there have been major changes and much progress. Things have come a long way since then. The discovery of electricity, automobiles, airplanes, rockets to space, men in space, two world wars. Yep. A lot has taken place."

"Wow. I definitely want to hear about all of that but I'm really interested in you telling me more. More about guys like you and me."

"It's been a struggle. Being like us had been illegal. As I'm sure you're well aware. They used to say we were mentally ill. We were put in institutions. But in June of nineteen sixty-nine, things changed. An event in New York City took place. A standoff between around fifty patrons at a bar called the Stonewall Inn and the police. It lasted almost a week. That was the turning point. It was the beginning of guys like us getting organized and fighting for rights. It was the start of the 'Gay Community' and the 'Gay Rights Movement'."

"Also, studies were being done by the medical and psychiatric community, finding out we are born this way. It's not a choice. This information became public in about nineteen seventy-three. Of course, there are those religious groups who disagree, still condemning us. It's sad. They don't get it and they never will. I feel sorry for them. It's really incredible. We as a group have come a long way. But there's still a long way to go."

"So, you can live together and no one says anything?"

"For the most part. As I've said, there are still a lot of folks who have no intentions of changing their minds regarding the subject even with modern knowledge. One thing is, they can't cause physical harm to us without going to jail for it. But most folks are understanding and have no problems. It's only those who remain ignorant, intolerant and uneducated and don't want to know the truth. Sad."

We were silent for a while as we watched the sun slowly slip below the western horizon. It was a beautiful sunset. Finally, night closed in. It was time to get in the boat and rest. Tomorrow we'd head out and continue our trip around the island.

We arranged the cushions in the bottom of the boat and got in, lying down. All was quiet except for the sound of the crashing surf.

After a moment, Brody whispered, "Goodnight, Mark."

I whispered, "Goodnight, Brody."

I couldn't help myself. I yelled out, "Goodnight, John Boy!" And I started to laugh.

Brody reacted, "What was that? John Boy? Who the hell is John Boy?"

I just laughed, "That's a story for another time. Goodnight, Brody."

"Goodnight, Mark."

After a few moments of silence, Brody yelled out, "Goodnight, John Boy! Whoever the hell you are!"

We both roared with laughter.

It was silent for a short time when Brody wrapped his arm around me. He whispered, "Good night, Mark."

I smiled and whispered, "Good night, Brody."

All was quiet as we finally fell asleep.

Chapter VII

I was awakened by Brody shaking me. "Hey. Time to rise and shine."

"Yes, I guess it is time to get the show on the road." I could tell by the position of the sun that it was late morning.

We gathered up everything from around the boat and arranged them neatly in it. Just as we were getting ready to get in, we heard a low rumbling. It got louder and louder. Then, the ground began to shake. Almost as soon as it began, it was over.

Brody looked up at the cone of the volcano. "Another quake. I'll bet the portal is open again."

We were lucky the tide was in, making it a lot easier to get out to open sea. I asked Brody to take over. We raised the sail and headed around the southern end of the island and then to the northeast. It was now obvious that the cone of the volcano occupied the southwestern end of the island.

Brody was excellent at handling the boat. He knew exactly when to shift the sail to catch the most wind. It was very clear I'd be 'leaving the driving to Brody' from then on. As we moved along, I continually watched the shore. I wanted to see if I saw anything unusual we might check on at a later date.

After a while, Brody spoke up, "What would you think about heading northeast and seeing what exists over there on the mainland?" He turned his head to the northeast. "It looks like I can see mountain tops far in the distance."

"I think we could do that. And you're right." I also looked in that direction. "Those are the tops of the mountains on the mainland. But if it gets hazy, we just would need to make sure we can find the island again."

"Well, if we use the compass and the position of the sun, we should be able to do that. We may be able to see the top of the cone from the mainland." Brody peered back at the volcano.

"That's true. And it's not like we're trying to sail halfway to China to find land. It's less than a day's trip northeast of here. I figure it's about twenty-five miles away."

Brody smiled, "I'm so glad you're here. We've done more in the couple of days you've been here than I have in the nine months I've been here. It's been great having the company, too."

I agreed, "If I had to be marooned on an island with anyone, I'm glad it's you. I enjoy your company and you're so easy to look at. Oh, yeah! By the way, you look great to be well over one hundred and fifty years old."

We both roared with laughter.

Brody was catching a great breeze in the sail and the boat was moving through the water at a pretty good pace. I had the fishing line over the side in hopes of getting something for dinner.

It was mid-afternoon when we rounded the northern end of the island and pulled ashore. We could see that the portal was open. I had also figured out that the island was about a mile and a half wide and around six miles long.

Unfortunately, I'd not been lucky at fishing, possibly, since we were moving so fast through the water. We hurriedly ran back to camp, filled the water jug and also drank our fill from the lake. No time was wasted in returning to the boat. Before going to sleep, we ate some of the fruit we had picked the previous day.

As we were ready to call it, there came a low rumble that grew louder and louder. The ground began to shake. Within a very few seconds, it was over. The shaking stopped and the rumbling ceased.

Brody looked to the northeast and then at me. "Wow. The portal is now closed. The one bringing you here was less than a week ago. They seem to be getting closer together and a shorter time staying open."

"Interesting. It could be just a little restlessness before going back to sleep again. Who knows?"

As I lay in the bottom of the boat, I began to reflect on the couple of days I'd spent on the island. Surprisingly enough, it had been more eventful than I'd expected. I also have to admit, it sure was nice to have the company of such a man as Brody.

———※∞∞◌◌◌◌∞∞※———

The next day, we got up early and Brody took me on a trek through the jungle to the south and west. It sloped down off the plateau to the sea and toward the woodpile. He wanted me to see where he'd found trees with edible fruit. I brought the picnic basket along to carry things we might find. Brody snickered, "If the birds are eating it then it's less likely to be poisonous."

By late afternoon, we'd gathered a nice basket full of goodies. I have to admit, I was sure the fruits were guava and papaya. I was just so glad they were edible. It meant we wouldn't starve to death.

Before ending the day, we went to the hot springs to get cleaned up and wash our clothes. We carried our wet clothes back to the boat and hung them on nearby bushes. We walked to the boat and got in.

Night was closing in as we lay there quietly. After a while, Brody spoke quietly, "I want you to tell me about John Boy one of these days."

We both just chuckled.

———※∞∞◌◌◌◌∞∞※———

I must interject here regarding going to the bathroom. Brody had pointed out a plant with large leaves that he would use to wipe himself. He would always do his bowel movements with no clothes on. After using some leaves to wipe himself, he would then run into the surf to clean anything remaining. Every time I went, I wanted to smack myself for not having toilet paper on the boat. Okay, now back to the story.

———·····———

The next day, we were up fairly early. We ate more fruit before heading out. We didn't want to spend too much time exploring as we wanted to get some fishing done, so we'd have something for dinner. Of course, we dragged the turtle shell and I brought the basket in the event we found some nice goodies to bring home.

We headed around the southern end of the lake and then into the jungle to the west. Brody said he'd never been in this area.

The edges of the jungle nearer the open area were rather thick with vegetation but finally cleared up some when we got farther into it. Shortly, we came upon a little group of lime trees. Brody took his stick and knocked several out of the tree which I placed in the basket. Then, we continued onward.

Suddenly, the jungle got thicker again. I was sure it meant we were coming to some type of clearing. Working our way through the growth, I discovered I was correct.

We came upon a good-sized area, almost half the size of a football field, where there was no growth. The whole space was covered with a volcanic lava floor. It was obvious nothing could grow there.

We paused and looked around. We looked up and could see we were closer to the base of the cone of the volcano.

On the other side of the clear space, I saw something that I could not believe. I pointed. "Brody! Look! I don't believe it! Pineapples!" It was a huge growth of wild pineapples. We now had something else to add to our fruit list. "Let's go get some." I said a silent thank you to all the birds who brought seeds from the mainland.

Heading toward the pineapple growth, Brody questioned, "What are pineapples?"

I realized he most likely had no idea what they were. "Pineapples are a tropical fruit. You're going to love them."

While crossing the clearing, I noticed a few birds come flying out of some bushes and vines, growing over near the face of a hill near the pineapples. "Besides the pineapples, I think I just might be able to find you some eggs." I headed in that direction.

Getting next to the bushes and thick vines, I started moving the leaves away to see into the foliage. That's when I felt a slightly cool breeze, coming out in my direction. This didn't make sense. There was no reason for such a thing to be happening. I used both hands to push the vines apart. The cool breeze continued coming out at me. "Brody! Come here!"

Brody walked over to where I was standing. I pointed. "Look. Feel that?"

Brody got closer to the place where I'd been pulling on the

vines. He held his hand up. He looked at me. "Cool air. There must be some hole here. Let's see if we can both pull some of these vines away."

He got on one side and me on the other and we began to pull in opposite directions. Slowly the vines gave way and we could see the entrance to a cave. The cool breeze was slowly coming out of the cave. The entrance was about six feet high and about five feet wide.

I looked at Brody with a big smile on my face, "Well, what do you think?"

"I think yeah but we really don't have anything to light the way. It could be too dangerous without enough light."

"Okay. Here's an idea. I know this may sound really stupid. What if we use the turtle shell, build a small fire in it and drag it with us as light?"

Brody clapped his hands together and tipped his head back with laughter, "Not a bad idea. I see your mother didn't raise a dummy. That's how I got the fire to the camp. Will tell you about that sometime."

"Right now, we can go in a little way and just look. Definitely, wouldn't want to get lost in there."

"Tomorrow we can come back here and use a fire in the shell as light. Great idea. Unless you had something else you were thinking about doing tomorrow." Brody looked at me.

I looked right at Brody then started looking around in an agitated fashion. "Wait just a sec. I'll check my pressing schedule and see if we can squeeze it in."

We both looked at one another in silence for a moment then broke out roaring with laughter.

Slowly, we walked into the entrance. Looking around, we could see it went into the darkness. Light was essential to go any farther. The cave was only about a leisurely hour from Brody's camp. We'd explore the cave the next day.

We immediately went to the pineapple growth and broke several off that were ripe. I commented, "We can use the knife to cut off the outer surface before we eat any."

We headed back to the beach. Brody got the fire up as I prepped a pineapple for us. Brody was quite pleased with it. "Wow. These are incredibly delicious. Nice and sweet. I'm really glad we found them."

Finishing the pineapple, we headed out in the boat to go fishing. Within an hour, I'd caught two fish and we headed to shore.

All the time we ate, we talked about what a fluke it was how we found the cave. If the birds hadn't flown out of the vines, I'd have never investigated for possible eggs. We were both very excited about exploring its interior.

Chapter VIII

It was early morning when we both woke up. Brody wanted to know if I wanted a few pieces of pineapple before we went on our outing.

I looked at Brody. "No, but I sure as hell would love a cup of coffee."

Brody bent his head down and just shook it.

We gathered up a good number of smaller pieces of wood and twigs, placing them in the picnic basket. I grabbed the lighter and put it in there as well. I'd collect dried leaves and more twigs along the way.

Brody grabbed his length of rope. He put his left arm through the loops, then over his head and onto his right shoulder. He also dragged the shell after placing a few small rocks, a layer of sand in the bottom and then several pieces of wood. The rocks and sand would help insulate the fire from the shell, reducing possible damage to it.

Finally, we were at the entrance to the cave. It was about mid-morning.

"Let's not light the fire in the shell until we really need light." I suggested.

"We can take our time doing this since it's new territory." Brody stared at the cave entrance.

We took our time entering the cave. With the cave entrance being only about six feet high, Brody, being over six feet tall, had to duck his head for several feet into the cave to make sure he didn't hit his head before the ceiling got higher. Soon, our eyes got accustomed to the darkness. It didn't take long for light to become necessary. I placed a pile of dry material in the turtle shell on top of the sand and stones. On top of that, I placed small twigs and small pieces of wood. Using the lighter, I lit the leaves. Soon, the small fire was going well. I was surprised at how much light it actually gave off. We headed deeper into the cave. We could feel the slight cool breeze coming at us.

In no time at all, the cave opened up into a larger cavity. It suddenly occurred to me, there was some sand on the floor. Not a lot. Just enough to fill places and holes to make the walking smoother. How is it that sand got all the way up here into this cave? I called out, "Look! There's sand on the floor. How did it get here?"

"That's a very good question." Brody stopped pulling the turtle shell.

I bent over, so I could see the sand more clearly. I walked up in front of Brody. That's when I saw them. "Oh, my God! Look! There are footprints in the areas where there's sand! They look like they were made by some kind of footwear. Possibly boots."

"You're shitting me! Footprints? Really!?" Brody yelled out.

"Damn! Someone has been here before. They must've been using this cave as a shelter. They brought in sand to make the floor a little less rough in places. I now have a million questions as to who they were, when they got here, how they got here and when they left." I couldn't believe it.

"Maybe they left some stuff behind. We need to really check this place out." Brody stared into the darkness ahead. "I'll bet they used a turtle shell like we've done to bring in the sand. Who knows?"

"I think you're absolutely correct. But let's go slow. I mean, you never know. There could be traps." I tried to be cautious. "I sure wish I had a flashlight right now."

Brody looked strangely at me. "A flashlight?"

"Yeah. For you, they haven't been invented yet." What could I say?

As Brody slowly dragged the turtle shell along, I added more wood to the fire, so we could continue to see. We finally came to where the chamber was even larger and continued farther into the darkness. Both of us were very careful to try and notice anything helpful to explain who once occupied the cave. We did notice the placement of sand was in a specific direction, so we followed it.

We went deeper and deeper into the cavern. I was pretty sure the cavern was caused by hot lava. I'd seen pictures of lava tubes at volcanic locations. This cavern was most likely one of these.

I looked into the picnic basket to see the supply of wood there. "Brody. Our wood supply is getting low. I think we should head back."

"This thing seems to go on forever. But you're right. We don't need to get stuck in here in the dark."

Suddenly, Brody stopped short. "Look!" He yelled, "There's some light ahead."

I walked up to where he was standing, so the light from the fire wouldn't interfere with my vision. I looked straight ahead. He was right. It appeared to be about a hundred feet away. The light was dim but it was there.

Brody looked at me and spoke quietly, "How's the wood holding out? Do you think we have enough to go check it out?"

I looked in the basket. "Okay. If we get there fairly quickly and we don't burn any more wood, I think we can do it. But we'll have to haul ass, getting out of here before we get stuck in the dark."

The sandy floor made it relatively easy to move a little faster. Within no time, we entered an enormous space. Located in the very high ceiling was a pretty good-size hole, allowing daylight to penetrate down into the space and was most likely the source of the air movement.

Brody started perusing the dimly lit area from left to right. "Wow. To really check out this place is going to take some time."

I tried hard not to laugh, "Wait! Let me check my schedule. No. No. I see no pressing engagements for some time now. I think we can squeeze this in." I looked at Brody.

Brody walked over to me, reached up, grabbed my hat and started hitting me with it. "I'll give you a pressing engagement. Yeah."

We both just stood there and broke out laughing. The sound resounded off the distant walls and ceiling. Brody handed me my hat back.

"I do think we should go and get something to eat. We can start this investigation tomorrow morning. How does that sound?" I suggested.

"You're probably right. I sure don't want us to get tied up in here and then it be too late to go catch some fish. We can start tomorrow."

Just as we were turning to head out of the chamber, my eye caught something in a dim distant shadow. "Brody! Wait a minute! I see something! Let's go look before we leave." We carefully headed in the direction of what I saw.

The closer we got, the more we both realized it was a wooden steering wheel and a ship's bell. Brody spoke quietly, "That's a ship's bell and wheel. For those to be in here, it is not a good sign for those who were on board. They are from a boat of fairly good size, too. I guess this definitely explains the footprints."

"I wonder how long they have been here and where did they come from?"

Brody looked around the huge space. "Further exploring may give us an answer. We can do that tomorrow."

"I agree. And we'll bring more small pieces of wood with us to keep the fire burning longer if necessary." I turned and headed toward the entrance. "Let me get a little fire started, so we can find our way." I placed some dry material on top of the embers in the turtle shell and some twigs on top of that. A small fire began to rise up. I placed some larger pieces of wood on top of that and soon we had light.

We both very quickly moved through the cavern and to the entrance. I warned Brody about bending his head down near the entrance, so he wouldn't hit it on the top of the cave. In no time at all, we were out in the clearing. Before heading back to the beach, we got a few more pineapples. Passing the lake, we filled the water jug.

Brody looked at me. "By the way, I've been meaning to ask. The water jug is definitely not glass. Is this another one of those plastic things?"

I looked at him with a big smile, "You are absolutely correct. It's a product that won't be around for at least maybe eighty years. Maybe a hundred years from your time period. A lot of stuff is packaged in it in my time. It doesn't damage as easily as glass does."

When we got to the beach and near the boat, I started the fire back up, so we could cook. After dumping the fire, sand and rocks out of the turtle shell, I looked at the bottom. It seemed the sand did prevent the shell from getting damaged. I was very glad.

Brody grabbed the fishing gear out of the boat and headed for some nearby rocks to start fishing. I returned to the boat and pulled out some larger pieces of wood for the fire. Once I saw it was burning well, I joined Brody out on the rocks.

Brody handed me the fishing rod. "Here. You do the fishing and I'll go take all the wood out of the boat and put it near where we have the fire. Then, I'll get us each a papaya."

I finally caught a fish. Our diet wasn't the best in the world but at least we weren't starving to death.

After eating, we climbed into the boat. With all the wood out of it, trying to sleep made it that much easier.

———— ∿∿∾ℰℸⓄⓄℸℰ∾∿∿ ————

After waking the next day, we both jumped in the ocean for a quick dip. It was almost a daily routine after going to the jungle and leaning against a tree if you know what I mean. Brody ate a few pieces of pineapple after I removed the outer area and cut it up. I wasn't hungry. In no time at all, we were headed off to the cave. I brought the picnic basket to carry wood and in case we found something we wanted to bring back. Of course, we prepped the turtle shell, so we could put a fire in it.

Once far enough inside, we built a small fire in the turtle shell for light. Very quickly we were in the large chamber since we now knew the way.

Brody looked around. "Okay. I think we should try to do this in some systematic fashion."

"I think you're right. That way we'll be less likely to miss something."

"What do you think of this idea? You go around that way since there's sand heading in that direction." Brody pointed in the direction to the right of the entrance to the large chamber. "And I'll go this way. There's sand in this direction as well." He pointed left. "That way we can kill two birds with one stone." He looked back and forth. "Not like this is going to be the last time we'll ever check out this place."

I agreed, "That sounds like a really good idea." I slowly started in my direction, staying close enough to the wall of the cavern not to miss anything. The light from the hole in the ceiling was dim but we could still see everything around us.

Brody headed in his direction. "Call out if you see something unusual."

Very shortly I reached the spot where the wheel and bell were located. I paused there for a few moments to look at them again. If they could speak, I wondered what stories they could tell. Continuing with my search, I saw nothing of importance. I called out, "I don't see anything more over on this side. How's it going over there?"

"So far, nothing. I do wonder about the ship and how many were aboard."

"Well, we've really just started checking things out. Maybe we will eventually find an answer. We need to just take our time."

Brody called out, "I just found another small cave entrance over here. We'll have to check it out. From what I can tell, we'll need some light to go in it."

I responded, "This big chamber continues in this direction but it's very dark in there and there's no more sand. I've gone as far as I can. I can't see anymore. I doubt there's anything farther on since the sand on the floor stopped."

"Well, I just found a fairly large area here covered with sand. There looks to be a lot of stuff over here against the wall of the cave. I have a horrible feeling that whoever was on the boat got stuck here." Brody called from across the chamber.

"Really? So, you think they never left?"

"Yep. There's a lot of stuff piled up over here against the wall. Looks like a bunch of personal stuff. A lot of old blankets and bedding. Looks like several piles of folded canvas. Probably from the sails of the ship. There's two piles of several folded blankets and believe it or not, two big turtle shells. With the amount of sand on the floor here, this area was probably used a lot. We need to save those shells, so we can use them in the future. I can probably carry them even as I pull the one we use for light."

"I'm going to head over to your side of the cavern as I can't see much farther here. I can carry one of the shells. That way you will only need to carry one." I slowly crossed to the other side while continuing to look to my right deep into the darkness beyond. There was no telling how far back the cavern went or what might be there. Reaching the other side, I saw sand on the floor again and slowly walked toward Brody.

Brody looked back at the cave opening he'd found moments earlier and then at the great darkness in the continuation of the main cavern. "Well, we have two choices. Which one do you think we should check out first?"

"How about your cave over there?" I stirred the coals in the turtle shell but not so hard as to disturb the sand underneath. Finally, the fire was burning brightly again.

Brody slowly dragged it and we entered the cave. We'd gone about ten feet when we came to a small room. When our eyes became accustomed to the dim light, we were very surprised at what we saw and realized.

"Damn." Brody spoke quietly, "It's a small burial chamber."

"I just counted. There are ten skeletons here. Eight of them are all lined up over there and they are all dressed in clothing, including boots." I pointed. "But there's something unusual about these two out here."

Brody looked at the two out from the others. They appeared to have been sitting and facing one another. He could see they were in some clothing, wearing boots and in the skeletal right hand of each one there was a knife. He continued speaking quietly, "Something tells me these two ended their own lives. Most likely at the same time the way they seem to have been facing one another. The others must've died first since they're all lined up in a definite pattern. I wonder what their story is?"

"Yes. I see the knives." I got closer to them, so I could see them more clearly. Brody joined me.

Brody shook his head. "It looks like the knives are the kind for hunting or fighting and look over there." He pointed to an alcove in the cave wall.

There was an organized pile of armor, helmets and swords. Further investigation revealed a pile of more knives. All were significantly rusted. I was sure it was due to the salt atmosphere on the island that passed through the caves.

It was perfectly clear to me after seeing the armor, helmets and swords. These were Spanish soldiers. I shook my head and spoke quietly, "Spanish soldiers. They are Spanish soldiers. They must have been on a ship that got them here and for some reason, they didn't leave."

Brody questioned, "But there are only ten of them. Wouldn't there be more?"

"Excellent question. You are correct. There should be more but where are they? Let's go look some more in the area where the bedding is located."

We headed out of the cave and back to the other area. While looking through the many things that were there, I came across a knife. This was not one made of metal like those of the Spanish soldiers. This one was different. "I found a knife and it's made of obsidian."

"Obsidian?"

"Yes. It's a type of glass. It's a volcanic glass. Obsidian was used by many cultures before there was the discovery of copper and iron. I have no idea why such a knife would be doing here." I handed it to Brody. "And be careful with it. Trust me. It is extremely sharp. We will take it with us as we sure could use a really sharp knife." Brody put it in the basket.

"What about the knives and swords in the cave?"

"Yeah. We can get a couple of the knives but I can't imagine why we would need any swords."

We quickly returned to the cave and got three of the knives from the alcove. I put them in the basket.

"I doubt the metal knives are very sharp because of the rust but I know the obsidian one is very very sharp. I now have something I can trim your hair and beard with. We'll make you look civilized again. What do you think?"

"Gee, thanks." Brody clapped his hands.

"Seriously. Obsidian knives are extremely sharp and will do the job perfectly. You'll see. We'll have you ship-shape in no time. I may even have to have you trim mine as well."

Just then, we started hearing a low rumbling and everything began to vibrate.

Brody yelled out, "Holy shit! It's another damn earthquake! Let's get out of here! We don't want to get trapped in here!"

"What about the turtle shells?"

"We'll get those another time."

Hurriedly, yet carefully, we made our way out of the cavern. Even though the shaking stopped way before we exited, we still wanted to get out onto open ground.

Finally, outside, Brody turned and looked at the entrance to the cave. "No need to press our luck. We should go see if the portal is open. I have a feeling it is." He shook his head then looked up into the sky. "I guess the gods aren't pleased that we took those guy's knives."

I looked at Brody. "Yeah. Right. Believe it."

We both shook our heads and snickered.

I turned to Brody. "Okay. I think we should go catch a fish or two, eat and rest up. We can always come back and check this stuff out."

"I think that's a great idea. Let's head back to the boat." Brody grabbed the rope to the turtle shell and we headed to the beach.

When we reached the beach, Brody stood there, peering out to sea. "Yep. It's open. I sure would love to know what's on the other side."

I stood next to Brody. "Well, you never know. But right now, I'm going fishing."

By the time I caught two fish and Brody had gotten the fire going, it was late afternoon. During the whole time, we discussed the group of ten, occupying the burial chamber in the cave. We could only guess, regarding their life and death. Brody thought since there was no way off the island for them, they had died of old age or some infirmity. Whatever the reason, it seemed that the last two had finally had enough and decided to join the other eight.

"I wonder when they got here and how long they were alive." Brody stared off at the horizon and the portal. "I sure would like to really know what happened to their boat."

"It may have been so badly damaged they may have just left it where it wrecked and salvaged from it what they could." I was just surmising.

"I have a feeling it was a pretty big boat and with no way to repair it, they probably did leave it where it wrecked. I'm sure over the years and with the surf, it just finally broke up and washed away or sank to the bottom."

"Yes. They could've been here for years. Since there is nothing but skeletons, it has been a very long time since they died and with the way the vines and vegetation had grown over the cave entrance. Maybe they came in during a storm and hit the rocks. I'm sure that would've done significant damage to their boat."

Brody turned and looked at me. "What if we're here for years?"

"Not going to happen. We're fortunate enough to have a boat. One that works. We can leave whenever we want. Our only problem is this. When we travel through the time portal we'll have no idea where we're going to end up. That could be very dicey." I looked out to sea in the direction of the portal. "Yeah. It's open right now. We could leave right now. But. What if? What if we ended up in Dinosaur World!?" The thought started me snickering. I looked over at Brody. "I'm sorry. You truly don't get the full humor of my comment. That's too bad. Because it really is kind of funny. Scary as shit. But funny."

"Dinosaur World. Something tells me if we were really there, it would NOT be funny."

Brody's comment made me slap my leg and put a big grin on my face, "Actually, you're correct. It definitely would NOT be a good thing."

It was dark by the time we finished eating and discussing the dead. We both continued to wonder what we might find farther and deeper into the large chamber. I kept wondering why Spanish soldiers were on the west coast of Mexico and how did an obsidian knife get into their possession. Little did I realize but the answer was going to become known in the very near future.

We climbed in the boat, positioned the cushions in the bottom and got in. We were quiet and finally asleep.

Chapter IX

I woke up, suggesting we head to the hot springs and get cleaned up. Brody was going to get his hair, beard and stache trimmed. When we got there, I had Brody sit on a rock for the process. Taking my time, I was very careful to make sure I didn't take any big chunks out of his hair and beard. The obsidian knife I was using was amazing and incredibly sharp. When I was finished, his beard was about an inch long. The hair on the top of his head was about two inches long and about one inch on the sides. I was afraid to cut too close under his chin for fear of cutting him. I'd never learned to use a straight razor and now wasn't the time to experiment. Before I even started, I made sure the knife was very clean, washing it in one of the hot springs. It was the same for the three metal ones.

I stood back, looked at Brody and smiled, "Damn! You really are one good-looking man. Geez."

Brody just looked up at me and grinned, "Well, I have to say. You really do know how to boost a guy's ego. Especially, a guy who is forty-two. Thanks."

I snickered, "Hey. From my standpoint, you're at least two hundred."

Brody just shook his head. "I swear. Can't even give a guy a break."

We both chuckled.

"Seriously. In my time period, guys who are your age… forty-one, forty-two…" I nodded. "They're the ones everyone is looking for. Hey. I'm thirty-nine and it's the age I'd want to connect with."

"Why wouldn't you want a younger guy?"

"Because I'd have nothing in common with him regarding life and historical experiences. Also, I would never base a relationship on sex. As my mother has told me, 'You never base a relationship on sex because you can't do it twenty-four hours a day and seven days a week. You better be able to talk and have fun with the person.'"

Brody looked at me, bent his head down and spoke softly, "Do you think you could ever consider connecting with…" He paused for a moment, "With. With me? I know we don't have anything in common, coming from two different centuries."

I shook my head. "Physically, you're definitely the kind of guy I'd look for. But I don't consider myself that good-looking. You deserve someone who's at least as handsome as you are." I paused for a moment and had to bite my lip from laughing, "But I must admit. Finding someone close to your two-hundred-year-old age would be extremely difficult." I broke into laughter.

Brody began laughing as well, "Damn! You can't give a guy a damn break over this age thing! I swear!"

"I'm sorry! I'm sorry. Yes. I do like you and I'm comfortable with you and so far, we work exceedingly well together. But I can't imagine a man like you being interested in someone like me."

"Mark, I feel so comfortable with you. I've so enjoyed the time we've shared together. And what's wrong with you? You're just the kind of guy who has always caught my eye."

I was totally bowled over. "This is quite funny. There's a very old expression, 'Beauty is in the eye of the beholder.' Maybe it is applicable here." I shook my head. "There was this old TV show back in the sixties called *The Twilight Zone*. Fantastic show. I'll tell you all about TVs another time and movies, too."

"I happened to see one of the episodes. It was about a woman who was having plastic surgery because she was deformed. Everyone thought she was ugly. All through the show, you see her all wrapped in bandages. You hear but never see the nurses or doctors. Finally, it's time to unwrap the bandages on her face. And when they do, you hear the nurses gasp, 'There's no change! There's no change!' Then, you see the woman's face. And she's beautiful. THEN, they pan out and you see the doctors and nurses. They, as we would think of it, are ALL ugly. It was a completely upside-down society. The name of that episode was 'Eye of the Beholder'. It was totally awesome."

Brody looked at me. "So. You see? Not everyone looks through your eyes."

"It takes me sailing out, landing on some remote mysterious island, caught in some stupid time warp, to meet an amazing and handsome man, who's from beyond the last century and who thinks I'm cool. What are the chances?"

Brody snickered, "Yes, I see what you mean. That is rather funny." He smiled, "Well, how do you think it is for me? Geez. There's no one like you back in eighteen fifty. You're open and fun and right upfront about it all. And personally, I think you're fine. What can I say?"

We gathered everything and headed back to the boat.

"Okay. We need to go check some more in the cave. I'm curious if there's anything more to find."

We gathered everything together to take with us to do further cave exploration. I even brought the obsidian knife. Brody brought the same twenty feet of rope he had before.

Before entering the cave, I ran over to the bunch of pineapples and used the knife to cut us two. On a nearby rock, I used the obsidian knife to cut them up. It would be a nice morsel before going in.

"Thank you." Brody ate his share.

Getting as far into the cave as possible, we then lit the fire in the turtle shell. I was glad the sand in the shell was eliminating damage to it.

Now, knowing our way, we hurriedly traveled through the cave and into the large dimly lit chamber. We quickly rounded the left side of the space and headed into the darker area on the other side.

Just before we entered the deep darkness, Brody turned to me. "Okay. Are you ready? Something tells me this may be all for naught. We do need to progress slowly, though."

We began by walking down the left side of the chamber. Its size began to diminish as we got farther in but it was still very large. It was large enough that we couldn't see across to the other side. Soon, we came across a small cave to the left.

"We'll check it later on." Brody commented.

We slowly walked for another fifteen minutes. We had virtually come to the end. At that point, a cave that looked to be about twenty feet in diameter went up at a very steep angle. It had to have had an angle of at least seventy-five degrees. Much too steep to climb.

Brody looked up into the darkness of the cave. "I doubt seriously anyone ever went up there. You'd break your neck, trying to do it."

I also looked up. "Yep, I totally agree."

Brody looked to his right. "Okay. Let's check out this side of the cavern." He led the way.

Very shortly, we came to a large recess in the wall of the cavern. Slowly, we walked into the area. There was something at the far end. We finally got close enough and even with the dim light from the fire in the shell, we could make it out. We walked closer until it became very clear what we were seeing.

It was another burial chamber. But this chamber was for someone special. The skeletal remains, dressed in clothes and boots, lay on top of an elongated pile of sand and rock about a foot and a half high. The skeleton had on a helmet, armor plating and a sword lying on its chest and stomach, being held by both skeletal hands. It had to have been a Spanish soldier of high ranking.

What also caught our eyes were the items placed around the pile and against the wall of the chamber. There were several large plates, bowls, several pitchers and several closed wooden boxes of all sizes.

Brody walked over and picked up one of the plates. He looked very hard at the plate then turned and looked at me. "This thing is heavy. I'd swear this damn thing was made of gold."

I picked up one of the pitchers. "Brody, my man, you are correct and so is this pitcher."

He walked over to the largest wooden trunk and slowly opened it. It was filled with what looked like clothing items.

I went and opened one of the smaller boxes. "Oh, my God! This box is filled with gold pieces."

Brody lifted the top piece of clothing from the trunk. He was shocked when he saw what was beneath it, "Holy shit! Look what I found!" He lifted up one of the items and turned it toward me. "It's some big green stone. And there are a lot more. Some of this stuff looks like jade and other stones and long pieces of gold here."

I looked over. "I'm not really sure but I have a feeling that rough green stone is not glass. And you should see all the stuff in this little box I have here."

Brody looked hard at the stone. "You think this stone could possibly be an emerald?"

"That's exactly what I mean."

"Damn! This one stone alone could be worth a fortune."

"You've got that right."

I quickly added a few more pieces of wood to the fire as the light was fading.

Brody continued to slowly go through stuff in the trunk. That's when he discovered a book. "Mark! I just found a book in here." He opened it and saw that it was handwritten. "It's not in English but I have a feeling it's a type of log book done by our gentleman lying over there." He turned toward me. "I think we should move this stuff to camp and see just what we've got." He looked over at the skeleton. "Do you think we'll go to hell for taking his stuff?"

I shook my head. "Well, if we get another shaking like yesterday, maybe we should reconsider. But I doubt it. Just like all the tombs in Egypt. The old expression is so true, 'You can't take it with you.'"

"I think we need to head back to camp and talk about how to do this. I think if we go back and get that big piece of sail canvas, we could use it to drag things out of the cave. Once the stuff's outside, we'll not need light anymore and we can use a turtle shell as well." Brody continued looking around the space.

"That's a great idea. The canvas should move fairly well on this sandy floor."

"Since we're here, let's at least grab a couple of things and take them with us now." He took the rope connected to the turtle shell and tied it to his belt. Then, he picked up several of the gold plates, sticking them under his left arm, a large bowl in his left hand and two of the pitchers in his right hand. In the pitchers, he placed some of the stones from the big trunk. He grabbed another bowl and placed it on top of his head like a hat.

I saw what he did. "That's a great idea. I'll put one on my head, too. I'll put this small box in the picnic basket and carry another box under my arm. I have to admit it sure is heavy." I looked back at Brody. "That's an awful lot of weight you're carrying. Are you sure you're going to be all right?"

"I'll make it. Once outside, I can put a lot of this stuff down."

I took my hat off and stuck the brim down in my pants. Then, I took one of the bowls and put it on my head like Brody had done. It was off to the cave entrance.

We continued on our way along the left wall of the cavern until we could see the light from the dimly lit area. Once there, we crossed the space very quickly and through the other cavern to the entry. Finally, out in daylight, I extinguished the fire and we placed several of the findings that Brody was carrying in the turtle shell. We headed back to the boat.

We placed all our treasures in the boat. We'd go through that another time. I wanted to do some fishing and catch us a few fish. Brody went back to his old camp and took down the canvas. He folded and placed it next to the path we'd take to go back to the cave. Then, he returned to the boat.

Brody got the fire started as I went out on the rocks to catch some fish. It took a while but finally, I caught one. Brody used one of the metal knives to clean the fish. He said that even though it was rusted, it was still sharp enough to do the job. We set up a few rocks around the fire and placed one of the large gold plates above it to use as a frying pan. There was no need to tie the fish to a stick anymore. We did have to watch, so the fire didn't get too hot and damage or warp the plate.

Brody had taken that gold plate and washed it off in the ocean. I knew that the heat of the fire would definitely kill any germs on the surface before we placed the fish on it. We would eventually take all the other plates, bowls and pitchers up to the hot springs to clean them.

I started laughing, "When was the last time you were cooking in a golden frying pan?"

All Brody could do was join in the laughter.

After we ate, we started going through our find. I opened the little wooden box and started taking pieces out, laying them on one of the cushions. There were several unusual pieces of gold decorated with colored stones. It didn't look like jewelry. I had no idea what they were. I did have a feeling the green ones were emeralds and some were jade. There was also a handful of loose stones and pieces of jade. Holding them up and looking at them for a while, I placed them back in the box.

Next, we opened the other wooden box. There were several pieces of what looked like gold bars in the box. That made me realize why it was so heavy. There also were several more large rough stones.

Brody snickered, "I think it's funny. We found gold, have become instant millionaires and have no place to spend our money."

I could only nod my head and giggle.

Before the sun went down, we took off our clothes and got into the ocean to clean up a bit. We didn't want to be in the water after dark because I'd always heard that that was feeding time for sharks.

We ran around a little bit on the wet sand, so we could dry off some. As we were running around, there came a rumble and shaking. Another quake hit. We both looked at one another and in unison spoke, "The portal just closed."

I spoke quietly, "You know we really do need to talk about the possibility of leaving the island and going through the portal. We could flip a coin and pick when." I paused for a moment, "Forget that thought. We don't have a coin to flip."

"I know we do but it is scary not knowing where we might end up and what we might have to face in that place." He shook his head. "But, we will. We will."

Then, we got into the boat. It wasn't long and we were asleep.

———∿∿◦⊙◦⊙⊙∿∿———

Another day began. We got up early, ate some fruit and readied to head to the cave. On the way, we picked up the folded canvas. Yes, we could have probably used one of the folded ones already in the cave but Brody already knew how he was going to use the one he had.

In our conversation about the occupants of the cave, we both agreed that it was rather fortunate that so many precious items had been removed from the boat after it wrecked. There must have been time making it possible and the boat had to have been situated to allow it to happen.

I told Brody that I would look at the book he discovered and see if I could make out what it said. If it was in Spanish, which I no doubtedly thought it would be, maybe there would be information as to where they were from and how they ended up here.

Once we were far enough inside the cave, I lit the small fire. We hurriedly moved through the cave and to the burial recess far inside.

Reaching our destination, Brody unfolded the canvas sail then refolded it again. This time it was folded into a rectangle about twelve feet long and three feet wide. Brody and I placed the large wooden trunk some three feet from the end of the folded canvas. It took both of us to lift it due to its weight.

Brody grabbed the corners of the folded canvas and pulled slightly. He turned to me and nodded. "I think I can pull it with no problem."

"There are several more wooden boxes here. Want me to put one more on?"

Brody looked at the several boxes still there. "Why not? How about that one over there." He pointed at one located next to the wall of the cave.

I walked over and picked it up. "Brody, it's kind of heavy."

"That's okay. Put it on anyway."

I placed the box next to the wooden trunk already on the canvas. Brody gave a tug. "Not a problem."

"I'll take a few more of these plates, another bowl and two more pitchers. No. I forgot. Someone has to pull the turtle shell."

Brody looked at me. "That's correct. Why don't you put those plates and a couple of the bowls on top of the big wooden trunk? That'll be enough for now. We'll be back for more."

"Okay. Are we ready? Let me get the fire going pretty good in the turtle shell." I took a few more twigs and a few pieces of wood out of the picnic basket and placed them on the fire in the shell. "That's it. Let's get moving." I led the way with a bowl still on my head and two pitchers in my hand that wasn't pulling the turtle shell.

We moved as quickly as we could through the cavern toward the entrance of the cave, being careful not to let anything fall off the canvas. We knew the path so well, it was getting to the point where I think we could've done it in the dark. Once outside the entrance, we took everything off the canvas and set them on the ground. I placed the two pitchers and bowl next to them.

Brody looked at me. "Want to go in and get some more?"

I gleefully responded, "Oh, hell. Why not!"

We turned around and headed into the cave, quickly heading to our destination. I was pulling the shell and Brody the canvas. Just before reaching there, I saw the small cave off to the left that Brody had found before. "Brody. Hold up."

Brody stopped. "What?"

"We haven't checked out this cave yet. Let me get one of those lit pieces of wood out of the shell and take a quick look."

"Okay. Just be careful."

I picked up one of the burning sticks out of the fire and walked to the small entrance. I held the stick out in front of me but it didn't give off much light. I took several steps into the darkness. With my next step, my foot didn't land on the expected floor. There was none. The floor level had dropped about a foot. Losing my balance, I let

E. Thornton Goode, Jr.

out a loud yell and began to roll into the darkness of the cave and down an incline. I'd dropped the stick and was searching through the darkness with my hands to find something to stop me. I finally grabbed hold of a rock sticking up. I did it just in time as my whole body, from my lower chest down, dropped off an edge. "Brody! Brody!" My mind went crazy wondering how deep the abyss was beneath me. "Brody! Brody!"

I heard Brody's voice coming from the dimly lit opening of the cave, "What happened? Where are you? Are you all right?"

"I'm hanging off a cliff. The floor is very uneven. I fell."

"Just a minute. I'll come get you."

"NO! Watch out! The floor drops off."

"Don't worry! Hold on!"

Several minutes passed and I didn't hear a thing. I was looking up and saw the light at the entrance to the cave got a little brighter. Brody must have put some more wood on the fire. Then, I saw him standing at the entrance.

"Brody! Be very careful! The floor of the cave slopes slightly then after several feet, it drops off significantly, like a step. That's where I lost my balance and fell."

I watched Brody get down on his hands and knees and began to slowly crawl forward in my direction. Suddenly, it was obvious he'd come over the slight drop-off. He was now moving toward me while crawling on his chest and stomach. In less than a minute, I felt his strong arms, reaching down, grabbing hold of me. He began pulling me upward.

I was afraid to let go of the rock. "Brody, I'm afraid. I'm afraid to let go. I don't want you to slip over the edge."

Brody spoke in a very deliberate voice, "I have you. Don't worry about me. I'm anchored. Now, reach up and grab hold of me and pull yourself up. I'll be pulling as well. Grab hold of my belt and pull."

Slowly and carefully, Brody pulled me high enough and over his shoulder, so I could reach and grab his belt. I pulled as he continued to pull me up and push me back. I worked my way across his back, grabbing his legs and moving toward his feet. That's when I realized he had the rope tied securely around one of his ankles. I grabbed the rope and began pulling myself toward the cave entrance, crawling slowly. That's when I felt him roll over on his back, sit up and start crawling behind me.

Finally, we were back out in the large chamber again. Brody untied the rope, put back on his boot then crawled over and grabbed me, pulling me close to him. He hugged me tightly and began rocking back and forth, "Don't ever! Don't ever do that again! I don't ever want to lose you. Do you hear me?" He grabbed my shoulders and pushed me back slightly. "Are you hurt? We need to get back outside, so I can see if you're hurt."

"I think I hurt my right foot a little. It hurts."

Brody got in a squatting position. "Put your arms around my neck and your legs around my waist."

I did just as he asked. With his left hand, he grabbed the rope to the turtle shell and stood up. Immediately, we headed in the direction of the cave entrance. He carried me in piggyback fashion. "Watch your head." He ducked down, so my head wouldn't hit the top of the cave. Once outside the cave, he let go the rope to the turtle shell, grabbed me tight and continued at a fast pace to the beach.

When we arrived at the boat, Brody turned around and backed up to the front of the boat. "Sit up there till I get a few things straight." He pulled off his boots and immediately maneuvered several cushions in the bottom of the boat. "Okay. Are you ready? I'm going to set you down on your good foot but I want to let the other one dangle in the ocean water. I can also check you out for some cuts. I see you have a nice one on your forehead. Brace yourself at the back of the boat." He lifted me up, walked me to the back of the boat and set me down, standing in the water. He put his right hand down into the cool ocean water then placed it on my forehead over the cut. He held it there for several minutes.

I turned my eyes toward Brody, "Yeah. I'll have to do this more often if this is the kind of service I get." I grinned then looked him up and down. "Geez. I knew you had a great build but I had no idea you were that strong."

Brody looked down at me, smiled then spoke quietly, "I just love how you make light of this. You could've killed yourself. If I remember correctly, I told you to be… careful. Damn."

"I swear I didn't see the floor of the cave drop down like that. But you're right. That stick didn't provide enough light for me to go farther. As the old saying goes, 'I should have looked before I leaped.'"

"I think that should be enough." Brody grabbed me and pulled me close to him. "Damn it. I'd have died if something had happened to you." He lifted me up, leaned over the edge of the boat and placed me on the pile of cushions. He put several under my foot to raise it up. "It looks bruised. You probably twisted it a bit when you fell. I'd like to take your shoe off but I have a feeling it will hurt like hell if I try. I want you to lay there for a while and later on, I'm going to take you up to the hot springs to clean you up and check you out."

I looked up from out of the boat. It dawned on me he truly did care for me. The realization I could've died made me also come to understand how my feelings were for him, "Brody." I paused for a moment, "Stay with me."

Brody looked down at me and smiled, "I'm going to go try and catch us a fish for dinner. Before we eat, we'll head up to the springs. When we get back here, we will eat then rest and I'll stay with you all night. Why don't you rest while I go fishing." He got the fishing gear out of the boat then headed off.

My ankle did hurt but I could tell it wasn't severely damaged. I managed to slowly take the sneaker off. I took the other one off as well. I lay there for a while and finally dozed off.

When I woke up, I sat up in the boat. My foot was feeling better but I saw I had really bruised it.

Brody saw me. "Caught two fish while you were resting. Cleaned them and put them in the picnic basket with fresh ocean water. Are you ready to go get cleaned up at the springs? I'll put our clothes in some of the hot water there."

I responded, "Sounds good to me."

Brody came over to the edge of the boat and turned around with his back against it. "Okay. Climb on."

I wrapped my arms around his neck and he pulled me up into a piggyback position. We were off to the springs.

When we got there, we took off our clothes and Brody put them in the hot spring. He put his boots over on a rock. Slowly, he helped me into the water. He used his hand to wash the water over my body to help clean it.

"All right. Turnabout is fair play. Turn around. I'll wash your back." As I used my hands to wash water over his back and shoulders, I also massaged them.

Brody groaned, "Damn! That feels really good. I'll bet you do this for all of your guy friends."

"Only the ones who are very, very GOOD friends."

Brody finally got out and pulled the clothes out of the hot spring, laying them on a rock to drain and cool. In a little while, he helped me out and we got ready to head back to the boat. Brody squeezed as much water out of the clothes as he could and asked me to carry them while my arms were around his neck. He put on his boots.

I grabbed all the clothes as Brody got into a squat position, so I could climb on in piggyback. It didn't take us long to return to the boat.

Brody put me in the boat then took all the wet clothes and hung them on the nearby bushes. He then went and stoked the fire, placing the clean gold plate above it, supported by rocks. Soon, the fish were on the plate and cooking. He used the fork to keep them from sticking and burning.

The sun was down by the time we climbed in the boat to rest for the night. Brody pulled me against him and wrapped his left arm around me. He whispered, "I don't know what I would've done if I'd lost you today. You silly goose. Don't you ever do something like that ever again."

I whispered back, "Thank you for saving me. If you hadn't been there, I'd have been a goner." I paused for a few moments, "Brody. All that stuff is still out there at the cave entrance."

Brody began to snicker, "Well, it's not like we have to worry about somebody running off with it. Do we?"

We both just chuckled.

Chapter X

For the next couple of days, I basically just took care of the cut on my head and my hurt foot. Okay, I did do the cooking. Brody did everything else. He also went and got all the items, sitting outside the cave entrance. When I was able to walk, we'd go back in and continue to get more. We placed almost all of the items we'd already taken from the cave into the boat. Only items we were using were not placed there.

The process reminded me of those going into the tombs in Egypt, taking out all the contents to put in museums if they hadn't been robbed first. It also made me think about the Egyptian religion. The high priests told everyone to put their belongings in the tombs, so they could take their stuff with them into the afterlife. What bullshit. LIES! And who gave the high priests this information? Ra? Osiris? Anubis? Yeah. Right! Hell NO! ALL religions were made up by MEN to control people and their money. There's no legitimate and unbiased proof ANY religion is from a god. No astounding, booming voice from the heavens has ever been recorded or witnessed by legitimate and unbiased sources. And if there had been, WHY are there so many different religions? A true 'god' would have the ability to eliminate all the 'fake ones', so that everyone would be on the same page. Got that? But what exists are a bunch of unfounded religions all claiming to be 'The One'. LIES! Total Bull SHIT! End of story. Suddenly, I was immediately pulled back to reality when I realized Brody was speaking.

"You know, I could go and get the rest of the stuff by myself." Brody commented.

"NO! You will wait for me. It's too damn dangerous to go alone." I guess I was being a little overprotective but I didn't want anything to happen to him. I couldn't help it but I was getting very attached to this man from another century.

Brody finally dismantled his camp and moved it down to the beach, so it would be closer to the boat. We no longer had to worry about fresh water. Having the water jug and several pitchers, it wasn't a problem to bring a substantial amount of fresh water from the lake in one trip.

—————wooccrocceoow—————

My foot eventually was feeling much better. We finally did go and retrieve all the items we wanted from the cave. Brody did virtually all the work pulling and dragging everything. I pulled the turtle shell with the fire in it. Almost everything was put in the front and rear compartments on the boat. The wooden boxes ended up in the bottom of the boat, under the seats, along the centerline to keep the boat balanced. Yes, we finally got the two turtle shells to use to get things.

Since we didn't need the canvas anymore to haul things, Brody took the canvas and stretched it over several pieces of wood he'd rigged up to form a shelter near the boat. Doing this was a good thing because one morning we looked out and saw a storm coming. He quickly got out the boat cover from inside the compartment at the bow and covered the boat. I took several of the gold plates and covered the fire.

The storm arrived within a few hours. It was nothing major. Actually, the rain cooled things off. Once it was over, I straightened things out to start cooking.

Brody decided to go diving around some of the rocks to see if there was anything available to eat besides fish. I watched him as he'd disappear beneath the water and after several moments, his head would emerge above the surface. After several tries, I saw him come up and yell out, "Look what I caught!" He waved a spiny lobster in the air. "Bring me the picnic basket. I'll put it in there."

I grabbed the picnic basket and as I walked out onto some of the rocks, I scooped up some water. I set the basket down and went back to the fire. I could tell my foot was getting significantly better.

Brody placed his catch in the basket and dove down for more. Soon, he had another. He climbed up onto the rocks, put the lobster in the basket and headed over to the fire. After I saw Brody had caught one lobster, I took one of the large gold bowls and supported it over the fire with some rocks. I took another large bowl, got some ocean water and dumped it in the bowl along with some fresh water, so it wouldn't be so salty. We could cook the lobsters that way.

As we sat eating, we talked about how well my foot was doing. Brody said the cut on my head was looking better, too.

As we ate the lobsters, I began to remember, "Do you know how much lobster is in Atlanta right now? The Maine lobsters are going for like sixteen dollars a pound."

Brody stopped eating, looked at the lobster and then at me. "You can't be serious."

"Yep. And God forbid you go order it at a nice restaurant. I won't even go there as to how much it would cost you."

Brody shook his head and changed the subject, "What would you think if we took a sail to the northeast either tomorrow or the next day?"

I clapped my hands. "Hell. Why not? We can really find out once and for all if Dinosaur World actually exists over there." I started laughing nervously.

Brody laughed, too, but I felt so sorry for him, not getting the total gist of the humor.

———∿∘०ए०⊙९०∘∿———

We didn't go the next day. We planned for the day after. Brody wanted to make sure my foot was feeling even better.

In preparation for the trip, Brody gathered a multitude of fruits and pineapples and filled the water jug to the top. I had the lighter ready and we made sure we had enough wood in the boat in case for some reason, we landed and wanted to spend the night. I also checked to make sure the compass was working properly. We would use it and the sun as directional beacons if necessary. All was now ready for our trip. We would get up early in the morning to go.

—⁓⁓⦿⊙⦿⁓⁓—

We did get up fairly early. I made sure Brody had a good covering of sunscreen before we pushed the boat out into the surf. We quickly turned it, so the bow was headed outward.

Brody helped me in the boat. After jumping in, he grabbed the oars and rowed us out to open sea. He raised the sail and we headed to the northeast. The wind was carrying the boat across the water at a fairly good clip. I was sure we'd probably see the shoreline within two hours. Since we were not going through the portal, the island would always be out there. There was no chance of us not getting back.

Brody told me to take a seat and just relax. He had everything under control. The sky was blue and filled with nice puffy clouds. It was as if we were on some leisurely outing. With all the treasure situated in the bottom of the boat and in the front and back compartments, its weight seemed to make the boat more stable.

I was correct. We began to see the distant mountains immediately. The shore on the horizon wasn't visible for just over what seemed to be two hours. Brody directed the boat straight toward it.

Brody tried to sound serious but I could sense a touch of humor in his voice, "As we get closer, keep your eyes peeled for any T-Rex dinosaurs on the beach."

We looked at each other and all we could do was just roar with laughter. Even though it was funny at the time, I still wondered what we would discover when we landed.

Several hours later, we both began to peruse the shoreline, searching for a decent place to guide the boat in. We wanted to avoid hitting any volcanic rocks. We sure as hell did not want to be stranded on the mainland in some unknown time.

What I found interesting is that I recognized the volcanic rock formations as the ones that were not far down from where my house was located. Of course, my house was not there just as no other ones were. We definitely were back in time before anything along the coast was ever developed.

Just before getting to the surf, he lowered the sail and grabbed the oars. Brody made a perfect hit near the beach. It was early afternoon.

Brody chuckled, "Okay. We're here. Do you hear any dinosaurs, coming through the jungle?"

I shook my head as I stepped out of the boat. "I sure as hell would love to know where we are in time."

Brody jumped out of the boat and walked up onto the beach where I was standing. "Well, we could walk up and down the beach and see if there's anything that could give us a hint."

"That we can do." I pointed. "My house should be right over there."

Brody looked to where I was pointing and then back at me. "What do you think? Should we go north up the beach or south down the beach?" He bent down and grabbed a small pebble from the sand. He put both hands behind his back. "I'm going to put the pebble in one hand and then bring both hands around. You're going to pick. If you pick the hand with the pebble, we head north. Now, are you ready?" He pulled both hands around and placed them next to one another.

I looked at both of his closed fists. Then, with the first finger on my right hand, being used as a pointer, I began. "Eenie... meenie... miney... moe." I looked at Brody with a big grin on my face.

Brody shook his head. "Okay! Okay! Pick a hand!"

I touched his left hand and he opened it. He grinned, "I guess we head north up the beach."

Brody grabbed the anchor and firmly embedded it in the sand. I grabbed the picnic basket in case we wanted to have something to munch on while we checked things out. We'd use the sun to get some idea as to what time it was. We began walking north.

Since we were near where the house was located in my time, we should have been able to see Lázaro farther up the coast. It's a huge port with giant cranes easily seen from a distance. There was nothing. Wherever we were in time, it had to be way before Lázaro came into being.

As we walked up the beach, Brody took note of the jungle to the right. There were no signs of a path or any other entry. "Doesn't look like this place is inhabited at all."

I jokingly responded, "Just keep your eyes checking for lions and tigers and bears. Oh, my!" I started to snicker.

Brody stopped short and looked at me. "Lions and tigers and bears?"

"Oh, my!" I shook my head and continued to snicker. "You'll have to move forward almost a hundred years and watch a movie called 'The Wizard of Oz' before you'll get that one."

Just then, we heard a rustling in the undergrowth. We both stopped and looked in the direction of the sound. A very large iguana slowly walked out of the jungle onto the edge of the beach and looked our way.

Brody looked at me. "Is that one of your dinosaurs?"

"Close! But no cigar!" I cried out.

Brody looked up in the sky toward the horizon, checking the position of the sun. "We should head back to the boat and I'll see if I can catch us a fish for dinner. You can start the fire."

Returning, Brody went out on the rocks and in no time at all, he'd caught a decent-size fish. He was cleaning it with one of the metal knives.

I gathered a few rocks to support the large gold plate above the fire. Shortly, we had things cooking.

After eating, we took off our clothes and got into the ocean to wash ourselves down. Night was beginning to close in. Standing on the wet sand, we attempted to dry off as much as possible before getting into the boat to rest for the night.

Lying there together, Brody spoke softly, "I wonder where we are in time? From your comments about there not being a town where there should be one, we are back from your time. I wonder how far?"

"I've seen nothing to give us a clue. Who knows? A hundred years? A thousand? What can I say? All I can tell you is that the rock formations are the same as in my time."

Brody pulled me close. "I'm glad you're here with me."

"Thank you for that. I'm glad I'm here with you, too."

There were a few moments of silence when Brody turned his head and yelled, "Good night, John Boy!"

Needless to say, we both just roared with laughter.

Shortly, Brody spoke quietly, "You know I'll never let that go until I know what it's all about."

I responded, "You will in time. I promise."

Finally, all was quiet and we were soon both asleep.

———$\cdot$∿∘◠◡◉◠◡◉◠◡∘∿———

One day not long afterward, I did tell Brody about movies and TV. He found them very interesting and indicated how much he would love to see them in reality.

———∿∘◠◡◉◠◡◉◠◡∘∿———

The next morning we ate some of the fruit we'd brought with us then headed south down the beach to see if there was anything to see there. We wanted to get back soon enough to head back to the island.

Brody stopped and turned, looking out to sea. "I think I see it. Yeah. I'm sure it's the very tip-top of the volcano on the island."

I looked to where he was pointing. It wasn't easy to make out but far out to sea, there definitely was something sticking up. "Damn. I think you're right. At least we won't have to guess. To get back, we now know exactly what direction to sail."

Our walk down the beach was fruitless as to finding anything to give us an indication where we were in time. So, we headed back to the boat and headed out. Brody pulled the oars and had the boat out past the surf in no time. Up went the sail and we were off.

It was evening when we arrived on the beach of the island. We ate a little more fruit before calling it a day.

I shook my head. "I'm so sorry we found nothing productive on the mainland. It looks like this whole place is in some uncivilized world, totally undiscovered."

Brody commented, "Well, this is our island and we'll make the best of it for now. We'll work together to make it our happy home. Until we decide to do something different."

"How about tomorrow we go back in the cave and double-check to make sure we got everything that's valuable?"

"Sounds like a great idea. And no side exploring." Brody looked at me with a stern expression.

I bent my head down. "Okay. I promise."

———————

As we finally took the time to go through all the things from the cave, we were amazed at the amount of gold in the form of ingots. These were not blocks normally associated with a gold bar but were lengths about eight inches long and looked to have been poured in a curved mold about an inch wide. These had been in wooden boxes stacked against the wall of the cavern in the burial chamber. Because of their weight, it had taken several trips to get them all down to the boat and placed in the bottom.

I pulled one bar out to look at it more closely and turned it over to see the curved side. I started to giggle.

Brody looked over. "What's funny?"

"When you look at the bar from this side, it looks like a gold finger." I paused for only a moment, recalling Shirley Bassey singing the theme song to the James Bond movie and started singing loudly, "'Goldfinger! He's the man. The man with the Midas touch!'" I couldn't help myself and broke out with laughter.

Brody shook his head. "Never mind. I know whatever it is, I'll have no idea what it is. But I'm sure it must be funny."

"You're right. And it is kinda funny."

One of the wooden boxes contained raw stones. They were in their natural state as if just discovered. Several looked like emeralds and were quite large, almost as big as your fist. There were other large pieces I was quite sure were jade. There were an assorted number of other raw stones. I wasn't sure what they were.

After examining our amazing discoveries, we placed everything back in their original boxes and placed them carefully back in the boat where we had originally put them. It was obvious from our trip to the mainland that the weight of the gold and other items did not unbalance the boat. We were smart to line them up and down the middle. The very large trunk was placed right behind the mast as it was a central position in the boat. The gold plates, bowls and pitchers we weren't using, we stored in the rear areas of the front and back compartments in the boat. I might add that we removed anything of real value from the large trunk and filled it with clothes and blankets from the cave. The logbook remained in it as well.

During several downtimes, I got out the book that was in the big trunk. Brody was correct. It was not in English but in Spanish and it was a logbook of information regarding the man who wrote it.

They were from Spain and exploring the new land, stopping in many places to see what was there and if it could be a place for a future settlement. It also told of encounters with local cultures in many areas. Time had been spent on the east coast but they had decided to explore even farther and sailed around the southern tip of the land. To me, this was obviously the tip of South America.

I surmised that they had had several encounters along the way with cultures that had treasure. How the treasure was obtained was never explained or even mentioned in the slightest. Since they had a knife made of obsidian, I was quite sure and it would be a good explanation that they had come in contact with a culture like the Incas.

It became evident why nothing was ever mentioned about discovering or obtaining anything of value when I finally read a section indicating that the book was to be turned in to higher authorities when the ship returned to Spain. I'm sure those onboard were planning to divvy up the treasure, telling no one of significance about it.

While coming up the coast of what we now know as Mexico, they ran into a major storm that blew them to the island and onto the volcanic rocks near the shore, severely damaging the ship. Luckily, there was time to get virtually everything of value off the boat before it was finally broken up by the wave action and the rocks. Heavy items just sank into the sea. This was interesting to me because it indicated that the storm was not only in the time where they had been but in the island time, too. What were the chances of storms happening in both places at the same time? Talk about major bad luck.

The man writing the logbook was obviously the one in charge. Although not typical at the time, he had had two lifeboats put on board their ship in case of some emergency. Everyone was so glad he did because it allowed them a way to escape the island and return to the mainland.

After exploring the island and finding the cave, they brought everything into the cave for safekeeping. Finally, it was decided that the head man as well as ten of his soldiers would remain on the island. The others would get in the lifeboats and sail to the mainland to get help.

After translating to English, this is one part that I found very interesting.

'We all gathered on the shore to bid farewell to our brothers. They all got in the boats and headed out to sea to the northeast. After a while, we saw they were about a mile out when there came a shaking of the earth. Just as it ended, we all noticed a strangeness out in the ocean. A very large area shaped like an arch started shimmering for a little while. We also realized the men in the boats were heading directly toward the middle of that area. We watched until we could no longer see the boats. I did hope they finally reached the mainland. I had no idea why there was a strangeness out there in the ocean but I did realize that the quake shaking must have caused it to happen as it was not there until the quake occurred. The next day I came down to see if the arch was still there. It was. I could see there was a difference between the sky in the area of the arch and the sky outside the arch. I was not completely sure what that meant. The thinking in my mind was too wild and insane to even consider. That there were two separate worlds was ridiculous. But as I stood there wondering, there came another shaking of the earth. At that same moment, the arch began to shimmer and after a little while, it completely disappeared. The area where the arch had been was now back to normal again.'

I knew immediately what had happened to the men who headed to the mainland. It made perfect sense to me when it was written that the men never returned.

Further information indicated that several of the remaining men got sick, including the guy writing the log. His last entry told of a few of them already dying and he was not far behind.

Finding all this out, I sat down with Brody, so he would be caught up on everything I discovered in the writings.

———⟋⟍⟋⟍⟋⟍⟋⟍———

Brody and I worked well together. This helped get things done quicker and left more time to just relax.

One morning as we sat there eating a few pieces of fruit, Brody snapped his fingers, "I have an idea. Why don't we take a trek up to the top of the volcano? I'll bet we could get an incredible view from up there. And who knows? We just might see other land or islands."

"Really? Wow, I think that would be an interesting trip. It might take a while to get there and back, so we better prepare. When do you want to go?"

Brody looked up in the sky. "It's early. We can start right now."

"Hey! Why not? I'll pack up the picnic basket and you get your rope and stuff and we'll head out. What route do you think we should take?"

"Let's head to where the cave is and go from there." He snickered, "That way we can get a couple of pineapples."

I chuckled, "Sounds like a plan to me. Let's get started." I knew Brody had become very fond of pineapples, having never had them before. I grabbed the picnic basket and started putting essentials in it including the obsidian knife.

Brody got his rope, filled the turtle shell with wood and he was ready. When this turtle shell began to show signs of wear, he planned to start using one from the cave.

It didn't take long to get to where the cave was located. I got several pineapples before we continued onward. We climbed the hill that went up and over the cave. The land around the volcano rose higher and higher. By late afternoon, we were at the base of the cone. I had a feeling we had traveled several miles.

Brody stopped and looked around. "How's this for a spot to make camp?"

"Looks good to me."

We began to prepare a small area where we could start a fire and have it as a base. It was obvious it wasn't going to be a cushy night for sleeping. I neglected to bring any cushions. Leaving everything at this base site, we decided to do a little bit more exploring. Brody had his rope looped over his shoulder, leading the way and I followed.

"We're not going to go too far. Just want to see how rough it's going to be to do the climb." Brody moved ahead.

It seemed to be about half an hour when we checked out possible climbing routes. I was surprised none of them seemed very difficult. We stopped at one point to check out the view. It was quite amazing. Virtually, the whole southeastern end of the island was visible. Looking to the northeast, we could just barely see the mainland. Some distance in from the edge of land, the mountains rose in the far mist. It should be very interesting what we'd see once we reached the top. Since it was getting late we'd do the climb to the top the next day. We headed back down to base camp.

I pulled several pieces of fruit and the pineapples from the picnic basket and handed some fruit to Brody. I found a nice flat rock to get the pineapples ready to eat. That done, I handed several pieces to Brody. Both of us also drank some water.

I looked at Brody. "What do you think? Should I build a fire?"

Brody smiled, "I don't think we need one. Shortly, it will be dark and we really should get some rest."

I sat down by a nearby rock and leaned against it. "Damn. This thing is really hard on the back."

Brody had positioned himself at another rock. He began to giggle, "I think my rock is smoother than yours. Why don't you come over here and sit between my legs and lean back against me?"

I shook my head and looked at Brody. "I don't want you to be uncomfortable."

"I'll be just fine. Now, get over here."

I got up, went over and sat down between his legs, leaning back against his chest. It was kind of like how we would be when sleeping in the boat. Only there, we were on our sides. This was much better and more comfortable. Also, Brody could wrap both his arms around me. "This is really nice. And it's very comfortable. Maybe we can stack up some cushions on the inside of the boat and sleep like this."

Brody pulled me close. "I think that's a great idea."

It was easy to relax. Soon, I was sound asleep.

Chapter XI

It was early morning when I woke up. I cannot lie. It felt easy and comfortable to sleep this way with Brody. The way he was breathing, I was sure he was still asleep. I slowly sat up.

As I did, Brody woke up quickly and with a start. He grabbed me and pulled me to him. "Are you all right?"

"I'm sorry. I didn't mean to wake you. Just thought I'd get us something to eat out of the picnic basket." I grabbed a guava and handed it to Brody. "You know, there hasn't been a tremor in some time now. Maybe this baby has gone back to sleep."

"I wouldn't bet the farm on it." He began to snicker, "What's the saying about the calm before the storm?"

After our quick breakfast, we began our trek to the top. Strangely enough, the climb didn't turn out to be difficult. We didn't climb straight up but in a spiral, first heading southwest.

This is when we saw Brody's woodpile. There was a ravine on the south side of the mountain. This is probably how hot gases escaped out of the crater, rolled down the mountainside and killed all the vegetation in its path. We soon saw the spot where the small flow of lava was still going into the ocean.

Circling around to the west side, we could see miles in all directions south, west and north. I stopped and was peering to the west. I pointed in that direction and shouted, "Look!"

Brody stopped, looking out to the horizon. "What?"

"I think I see it!" I yelled.

"What!? What!?" Brody questioned.

"Hawaii! I see Hawaii!" I turned my head as I began to snicker, "Just kidding! Just kidding!" I wasn't even sure if Brody would know what I was talking about.

Brody walked over, took the cap off my head and started hitting me with it on my back and shoulders. "Yeah. I'll show you Hawaii. Yeah. After I beat you to death. I'll show you Hawaii all right." Then, he handed the cap back to me and just shook his head. "I swear. I'm so glad you have a good sense of humor. But. Just wait. I'll get you back somehow. Yeah. Just wait."

"I wasn't really sure if you knew what I was talking about. The islands of Hawaii didn't become a state until the late nineteen fifties if I remember correctly."

"Yeah. I'd heard a little about them since some folks have gone there already from the States. I did know it was some islands way off the west coast."

Actually, there was no evidence of any landmasses in those directions. Not even the sign of distant mountain peaks. Halfway up the cone and reaching the northern slope, we could clearly see the land to the northeast that we had visited several days earlier.

I commented, "This is like being on top of the Empire State Building in New York. The view from up there is unbelievable."

"There's a building in New York City that's this tall?" Brody was surprised.

"Yep. It was the tallest building in the city until the World Trade Center was built. I never got to go to the top of either of those two towers, before they came down in two thousand and one."

"They were torn down? Why?"

"Oh, it was a terrorist attack. Two airliners were hijacked and flown into the buildings and they both collapsed. Several thousand people died. It was terrible."

Brody spoke with an angry tone, "Oh, my God. You're going to have to tell me more about that when you want to take the time. From what you keep telling me, the future is filled with wars, death and destruction. What is wrong with the people in your time?"

"You know, you're so right. People just can't seem to get along with one another. It's sad."

We kept climbing. It was early afternoon when we finally reached the top of the cone, peering down into it. I turned to Brody. "I'll bet we are at least twice the height of the Empire State Building now. Yeah." I looked into the crater. "How wide do you think the crater is?"

Brody tilted his head to the side as if searching for an answer. "I'd say it was about three hundred feet across. Maybe a hundred feet deep."

"Yep. That's what I thought. It looked to be about the length of a football field in width."

Brody's face took on a questioning look, "A football field?"

"Yep. A football field." I paused.

"Okay. Let's hear it but I already know what you're going to say." Brody grinned.

We both spoke in unison, "For you, it hasn't been invented yet." Then, we both just couldn't help but laugh.

Brody shook his head. "I am so glad you find this so amusing. At my expense. Geez." He grinned, "That's okay. I'll get you back. Just wait."

From where we stood and then walking around the top of the crater, it appeared the island was about six miles long and maybe a mile and a half wide. What I had thought originally, after our trip around the island, was correct. The volcanic cone sat on the southwestern end of the island. The visual made it very obvious that we were correct. The island was situated perpendicular to the mainland. We also realized that the portal was located between the island and the mainland and about two to three miles out from the island.

Something very interesting was a very large protrusion, coming up from the floor of the crater. There seemed to be slight wisps of steam, periodically issuing from the protrusion.

I looked at it with great skepticism and felt somewhat nervous inside. "I hate to tell you but this just reminds me of Mount St. Helens in the late nineteen seventies or early nineteen eighties. Can't remember exactly. I know I was only a young kid back then. It was all over the news at that time."

Brody had a questioning expression on his face, "Well, what happened?"

"A mountain that had sat dormant for what seemed like forever, woke up and blew half of Washington away when it exploded. It was not pretty. We may have to be more vigilant with this thing."

Brody looked at me with a funny expression, "Come on. Everyone knows there's no damn volcano near Washington."

I was totally surprised, "Oh! No! Not THAT Washington. Washington State. It's in the far northwest corner of the country. Two states north of California. But of course, in your time, it wasn't a state yet." I shook my head. "Brody. A lot of stuff has happened since your time. A lot."

"Really? I knew there was a mountain range way out west but I had no idea there was a volcano out there."

"Actually, there's a chain of them. And a supervolcano, too. Yellowstone. But being here on an island reminds me of another volcano. What happened there was not good at all."

Brody wanted to know. "What are you talking about?"

"The island of Krakatoa. It was located in Indonesia. In your time, that part of the world was called the Dutch West Indies. Probably the most noted volcanic event in modern history. In the summer of eighteen eighty-three, it woke up and the whole island exploded out of the ocean. It is considered to be one of the largest volcanic explosions in recorded history. And when it happened, it created a tidal wave around a hundred and twenty feet high."

Brody was shocked, "Damn! A hundred and twenty feet high? That's like a twelve-story building."

"Yep. Exactly. And the tidal wave killed like thirty-six thousand people. I don't think there has ever been another tidal wave as high as that one, since."

"Thirty-six thousand people! Wow!"

"Hey. There was a tidal wave out in that area just ten years ago. Caused by an earthquake under the ocean. Killed over a quarter-million people. It's amazing the number of people who live near the oceans of the world."

"But the one I'm waiting for is going to be caused by an island over near Africa. La Palma. That's right. The island of La Palma. I saw a documentary about it on TV. I'll explain what a TV documentary is another time. The Cumbre Vieja volcano is there. When it goes, they said about twenty-one cubic miles of earth will slide into the Atlantic Ocean. It is going to create the mother of all tidal waves. And it will head right to the eastern coast of the United States. Florida will get totally wiped out and so will New York City. It's the kind of wave they make movies about. Yeah. I think the documentary said the wave would be like three hundred feet high. YeeeHaw!" A bold expression filled my face.

Brody just looked at me with a questioning expression, "You amaze me. You describe situations where thousands have died and there's sympathy in your voice. But then you talk about a catastrophe killing millions and you make light of it. What is that?"

"It's probably because the latter sounds so unbelievable and it hasn't happened. It's like a fake movie in my head. So, it's not real."

"Okay. I kinda get it. You're going to have to tell me more about movies and TV sometime. From what you have told me about them already just makes me want to know more."

"I will. I could talk for hours and hours telling you about stuff that will happen and become a reality."

Brody looked in all directions down from the volcano. "From up here, there doesn't seem to be anything of major significance on the island. I think we've probably found the most important things in the cave."

"I think you're right. We can do some more exploring on the northern side of the island. We might find more fruit trees there. Other than that, we're here and this is it. As I've said before, our only major decision and I say major because it is very significant. Do we stay on the island, do we go and move to the mainland or do we finally decide to sail back through the portal when it comes up? We should talk about all the choices and we have to be honest with one another, regarding what we say. As I've said it before, if we choose the portal, once we go through it, there will be no turning back. It may never show up in that time period again."

"You're right. Since there's a boat, we're not stuck here but choosing one of the other two options does have its consequences." Brody tilted his head.

"You're right there. Let's go down and head home. Maybe if it's not too late, you can get us a few lobsters." I grinned.

Going down was much faster than coming up. We weren't sightseeing along the way. When we reached our little camp, we grabbed the picnic basket and turtle shell and kept going.

When we got back, we decided to go by the hot springs and take a good quick bath. By the time we reached the boat, it was too late to get in the ocean. I was afraid Brody could get eaten by a shark. We ate the fruit we collected on the way back.

Sitting by the small fire on the beach, we watched the night close in around us. I started telling Brody more about movies and TV, including popular shows and films. Of course, that conversation brought in a mention of the telephone. I told him we'd save that for another time as well.

Since we both were tired from our trip, we climbed into the boat and rearranged the cushions, so I could lean back against Brody's chest and sleep. Brody liked the idea as well.

It didn't take long and I was asleep.

Chapter XII

About what seemed to be almost two months went by as we got into a routine. I was doing most of the cooking and fishing while Brody went hunting for fruit. Only a few times did Brody go for wood by himself with a turtle shell. Most of the time, we took the boat and filled it up. Brody would periodically dive down and catch some lobsters.

Several times at the hot springs, I trimmed Brody's hair, beard and stache. He even started trimming mine since it had begun to grow out. He was so worried about how it might look. I told him I didn't have to see it, so it wasn't a problem. That made us chuckle.

What was very interesting is there had been no tremors during that entire length of time. None. Maybe the giant had gone to sleep again. Of course, it meant the portal didn't open, either.

———ᨖᨆᨆᨆ———

We'd finished eating our little morning meal when Brody made a comment, "I'm going to run into the northern jungle and get some more fruit. I'll also run by the cave and get us more pineapples. See if you can catch us something good for dinner." He went off, dragging a turtle shell.

After taking some things to the springs to wash them, I came back and climbed out on the rocks to do some fishing. To make it comfortable, I brought a cushion to sit on. As I sat there, I began to start thinking about what might be happening back in my real life and spoke quietly to myself, "I'll bet they think I'm dead. I should've been back at work long ago." I began to recall the Mark Twain comment, 'The reports of my death have been greatly exaggerated.' "Oh, well, there's nothing I can do about it right now." I shook my head.

What was really funny is there was no one who had the authority to close bank accounts, stop payments and things like that. Because of that, money from renters would still be able to be deposited into the Mexico house account and auto-payments would be made on the loans and expenditures. I was glad of that. There would be no defaulting on loans for the Mexico property.

It was quite a different story for the house in Atlanta. That money was coming out of my personal bank account where my paychecks were being deposited. Are you getting the point? 'No worky... no payey.' And of course, there would be no insurance money for over seven years after they finally declared me dead. I had to laugh to myself. It's amazing how much shit we have wrapped up in our lives.

If the house did get foreclosed on, I would hope my brother would put all my stuff in storage and not sell it off. With talks I'd had with him about the value of the art and antiques, I have a feeling he'd see to it nothing happened since it was so unclear as to my death. Hopefully, I was just a missing person. But if my stuff did get sold, well, *c'est la vie.* I just hope he gets what it's worth. What can I say?

Then, I began to think about the guys up in the cave. How sad. Having to remain here for their whole lives and all those elsewhere wondering what happened to them. I also wondered about the ones who left in the lifeboats and where they actually ended up after going through the portal. I hope they didn't end up as tasty treats for dinosaurs. Yep. Sad. And it was the same for Brody. His building supply and farm equipment company taken over by others would all be gone by the end of the Civil War. Burned to the ground. And here both of us sit with a king's ransom in precious and semi-precious stones and a slew of gold bars. I just shook my head. "It's ironic."

The fish weren't biting. I got up and moved to another rock. Maybe it would be better there.

It was early afternoon when I saw Brody coming up the beach. Getting closer, I could see he was holding a bunch of wildflowers in his right arm and pulling the turtle shell with his left. He had a big smile on his face.

Soon, he was close enough and I called out, "What's that? What are all those flowers for?"

Brody just had a big grin on his face when he walked up to the edge of the water. "Come off that rock and get your flowers."

I was astounded, "Brody! For me? But why?" I climbed down off the rock and walked up to him.

"These are for you. It's the only way I know how to tell you how much I've enjoyed our time together. The days we've shared have been the best days of my life." He grabbed them together and handed them to me.

I reached for the flowers with tears streaming down my face. "How thoughtful. How considerate." I looked up into his face. "I, too, have enjoyed the time we've been together. Even in this situation, I've been happy because of you. Thank you so much." I hugged him tightly. After a moment, I looked around. "Where is one of those gold pitchers? I can put them in one."

I couldn't deny it. Every day I felt closer and closer to Brody. Being with him was comfortable. He made me feel good. He made me happy. And I liked it.

As we lay in the boat to sleep that night, I whispered, "Thank you so much for the flowers. You have no idea how much it means to me."

Brody pulled me close to him. "I'm glad you like them. You have no idea what YOU mean to me."

We were quiet and finally asleep.

The next day it began to rain. All the hatches were battened down and we took refuge under the canvases. We'd moved many of the cushions under the canvases. Even our small cooking fire was now under the coverings and located at one end, so not to catch anything on fire. We had gotten one of the larger pieces of canvas that was folded up in the cave. Brody used it to reinforce the one he already had to make sure there were no leaks during a rain.

It rained on and off for three days. It was rather nice. It cooled things off considerably and it gave Brody and me downtime to talk about things. I told about so many things that came to be in the last hundred and fifty years. He was really impressed with what airplanes were and automobiles and trucks. He laughed when I explained about the plastic credit card and the consequences of not using it diligently. Yes. We totally enjoyed those leisure times.

———ɯɯ◦ᴏᴏⱸᴛᴏᴏᴛᴇᴏᴏɯ———

After a few days of rain, we decided to take another trip over to the mainland. Now, knowing it was not Dinosaur World, we wouldn't have to be constantly on the alert for a T-Rex.

This was our plan. Instead of walking up and down the beach, we'd sail up and down the coast. It was going to be a four-day trip. The first day would be sailing over and setting up camp. The second day would be sailing up the coast and returning before nightfall. The third day would be sailing down the coast and returning before nightfall. Day number four would be sailing back to the island.

———ɯɯ◦ᴏᴏⱸᴛᴏᴏᴛᴇᴏᴏɯ———

When we came ashore on the mainland, it was in the same

place we had landed on our previous trip. Of course, we brought our picnic basket full of fruit, Brody's length of rope, the turtle shell, the obsidian knife and the three metal knives we'd found in the cave. Several of these items were already being stored in the two compartments of the boat.

Upon landing, the first thing on the agenda was to build our fire. As I was doing that, Brody tried his hand at fishing. Within no time at all, he'd caught a fairly large one. After eating, we decided to rest early. It would allow a good day of sailing the next day.

———❦———

Sailing north up the coast, we continued to watch the shore to see if there was any sign of people. Nothing. All we could see was thick jungle beyond the beaches. Actually, we weren't surprised. I think we would've been truly shocked if we'd seen evidence of civilization. We returned to camp by early evening.

It was the same the next day when we sailed south down the coast. Returning to camp, we did discuss the possibility of moving to the mainland. There could be significant advantages to being there. Maybe on a future trip, we'd make an effort to explore inland and maybe even climb one of the distant mountains to see what we could see. It wasn't out of the realm of possibilities. Since we would still be in the same time as the island, the portal would always be available to us as a possible future move to another time.

The next day we packed everything in the boat and headed back to the island. The major disappointment we shared was the knowledge of knowing there was no hint or indication as to where we were in time. All I knew was that it was sometime before civilization came to this area of Mexico.

The last conversation we had before calling it a night was begun by Brody, "It's very interesting. It's been some time since we've had a tremor."

I responded, "I know. I'd thought the same thing. Maybe this thing has gone back to sleep. Every story I heard about a volcano indicated they went through phases of activity and dormancy. It could be going dormant again."

"Well, if it does, I hope it doesn't affect the hot springs. They sure are great to wash the clothes and take a bath now and then."

"Only time will tell." I shook my head.

We covered the fire with one of the large gold plates to prevent any sparks from popping out and maybe setting something on fire. Then, we got in the boat. I have to admit I was extremely comfortable at night with Brody lying there with me.

Chapter XIII

It was so funny. No cell phone. No TV. No computer. And I didn't miss any of it. Life was simple and uncomplicated. Brody and I took care of one another and that was all that mattered. It was great. Our diets were not the best but we weren't starving. We both did joke now and then about having a good steak.

Even without the amenities I always took for granted, I couldn't complain. Sharing time with Brody was a blessing. It was interesting to hear his stories from his time. I loved the information he told about my ancestors who lived at Whitby Plantation. Some of the hardships that existed from his time had been resolved and were no longer a problem in my time.

We even continued to discuss the fact that there had been no tremors opening and closing the portal. Perhaps the volcano had gone to sleep and we were destined to stay in the time we were in after all. With the boat, we still had access to the mainland and we continued to talk about the possibilities of moving there.

Time and days were passing but I really didn't take notice. I guess if I added up the number of times I had trimmed Brody's hair, beard and mustache and he had trimmed mine then did a little calculating, I'd be able to tell you how long I'd been on the island. With no change of season and temperatures, one day was like the previous one. Yes, there were a few storms now and then but nothing extreme. But if it was necessary to tell you, I'd say at least several months had passed by. So, if using my time as the mark, it was most likely June or maybe early July back home.

———✶———

The sun had just come up. It was going to be a bright sunny morning. We got up really early and ate a few pieces of fruit.

"Give me the water jug. I'm going to go to the woodpile and get some wood in the turtle shell. I'll stop by the lake and fill it up." Brody reached for the jug.

"Are you sure you don't want to take the boat? It's easier than walking." I suggested.

"I really don't mind. Hey. Why don't you come with me? Bring the basket. We can get some fruit along the way."

"Oh, hell. Why not. I'm not doing anything pressing."

I gathered up the jug and basket. Brody put his rope over his shoulder, grabbed the rope to the turtle shell and we were off. As we stopped on the large plateau area where the lake was and began to fill the jug, there was a strange low vibration in the ground. It lasted what seemed to be about thirty to thirty-five seconds. It made the surface of the lake shimmer.

Brody quickly looked at me. "Did you feel that?"

"Yeah. I did. But I didn't hear anything. Weird."

Just then, we noticed flocks of birds, flying up, leaving the jungle and taking to the air. They headed to the northeast.

Brody stared at the birds all flying to the northeast. "I wonder what that's all about? Looks like they're headed to the mainland."

"I've heard animals can tell when there's going to be an earthquake or other pending natural disasters."

"Well, there have been all those tremors in the past and they never reacted like that." Brody shook his head.

"With us being out in the open, I don't think we have anything to worry about. If it's a big one, we may lose our balance and fall on the ground. That would be about it. Big deal."

"Yes, that's true. Maybe it'll get the hot springs really going. We can take a really hot bath when we get back." Brody clapped his hands.

I just snickered.

Brody filled the jug, I stuck it in the picnic basket and we were on our way again. We were traveling at a leisurely pace since we were in no hurry.

If only we'd taken heed of the birds and realized the warning they were giving us, we didn't know it but it was significant. A significant change was about to happen in our lives.

We hadn't even left the plateau to take the path down the side of the hill to the woodpile area when there came another soundless low vibration. We stopped.

Brody looked around. "There's another one. In all the time I've been here, I've never experienced anything like those before."

"This is going to sound stupid. But, it's like the place has the shivers." I just looked all around.

"Hey. Good way of putting it." Brody looked around as well.

That's when I noticed there wasn't the slightest sound. If not for the slight breeze, you could've heard a pin drop. "Do you hear that?"

"What? I don't hear anything."

"Exactly. That's my point. Nothing. Not one sound. Not one bird is chirping. They must have all left. Maybe this is going to be one dilly of an earthquake." I was rather nervous.

After a moment's pause, we continued on our way. Down the sloping pathway to the edge of the dead area and down toward the beach.

We'd been joking and kidding around for about thirty minutes. Brody had taken his length of rope, thrown it up into some of the limbs, pulling them down for us to break into smaller pieces. We'd finally collected a whole turtle shell full. He'd indicated he was getting hot and took off his tattered shirt, hanging it on a nearby dead tree.

I had walked in the direction of the pathway to the slope, collecting smaller pieces of wood, putting them in the basket. That's when it happened.

It was a rumbling, followed by a huge deafening explosion. The ground shook so violently, I fell down. It was so frightening, I instinctively started running and crawling up the path on the slope and out of the dead area. That's when I turned and looked down toward Brody. He had fallen and rolled down toward the beach. I couldn't believe how tremendous the quake was. Strangely enough, I still had hold of the picnic basket.

I turned, sitting on the ground and yelled out, "Brody! Brody! Are you all right!?"

Brody had stopped rolling and finally sat up. "Yeah! I'm all right! Wow! That was a doozy! Holy cow!"

At that, there came another violent shaking that was worse than the previous one. Accompanying the shaking was an incredibly loud and almost beyond deafening explosion. I turned and looked up toward the top of the volcano. A huge column of black smoke and ash shot straight up into the sky. It was frightening.

At the same moment, right in front of me, a crack began to occur in the earth all along the edge of the dead zone from up toward the volcano and down toward the beach. As the shaking got worse, the crack got longer and wider. Within an instant, it was wider than five feet. I had to scramble up the pathway to keep from falling into it.

Suddenly, hot lava began to ooze up in the constantly widening crack and started flowing slowly toward and into the ocean, causing great clouds of steam to rise in the air. The crack had done a terrible thing. It had separated Brody and me.

As I looked down toward Brody, still sitting on the ground, there came another huge explosion from the top of the volcano. The sound of cracking and crumbling stone filled the air. "BRODY! BRODY!" I screamed out.

Brody quickly stood up, bracing himself against one of the dead tree stumps. He yelled, "MARK! GET OUT OF HERE! Leave! I think this whole thing is going to blow! Run! Get to the boat and leave the island!"

My heart began to scream as I heard him yell those words. There was no way I was going to leave him. I yelled back, "BRODY! I can't leave you! I can't leave you!" There had to be a way.

Brody called out, "There's no way I can cross the lava! You must go! You have to leave me! Go! Go! Save yourself!"

It finally hit me. Brody was not just another person, another man. I loved him. Over the time we'd been together, not even thinking about it, I had fallen in love with him. Through tears, I cried out, "Brody! I'm not leaving you! I love you!"

Brody looked at me, smiled and shook his head, "I love you, too! You silly goose! Now, get going! You're wasting time! You need to get away from this island! I want you to live!"

"Brody! I'll come and get you! You get down to the beach! I'll get the boat and sail around and get you!"

"There's no time! There's no time to come in the boat! You'll get killed as well!" He stood there shaking his head.

"I don't give a damn! I'm coming to get you! Get your ass down to the beach! Hurry up! I'm not taking 'NO' for an answer! And when the ash begins to fall, do NOT breathe it in. It will kill you."

I stood up and started running up the pathway toward the plateau. I actually shocked myself at how fast I could move. Even with the shaking of the rumbling earthquakes, I was traveling at a rapid pace. I don't think I'd ever run so fast in my life. Well, I'd never tried to run from an earthquake like this ever before in my life, either.

In no time at all, I was at the plateau and running to the other side. The earthquakes were causing the lake to splash out of its banks. I kept running. Finally, I was on the beach and the boat was in sight. I did notice the wind was blowing to the north. This was a huge plus in our favor, regarding the ash fall. At the present time, the south side of the island was safe from its fallout.

As I raced to the boat, I passed the fire, picking up the golden plate and pitcher, sitting next to it. Throwing them into the boat along with the picnic basket I was still holding, I yanked the anchor out of the sand and threw it into the boat as well. I was so glad the water was high enough. I pushed the boat with all my strength to get it out into the surf. It seemed my fright had given me super strength.

Quickly, I pushed the bow, so it was facing open water, climbed up the side and jumped in. I grabbed the oars, braced myself against the seat and the mast and rowed like I'd never rowed before. Shortly, I was beyond the surf and into open water. I quickly put the oars down and rapidly raised the sail.

Crawling to the back of the boat, I grabbed the rudder and headed southwest. Because of the wind direction, I knew I'd have to do some zig-zag tacking to get to the woodpile. It did please me the boat was moving along at a decent pace. All the time I couldn't stop looking toward the volcano and seeing the black column of smoke and ash, rising higher and higher into the air. I also could see hot, thick lava, beginning to emerge from the top of the cone and starting to slowly move down its sides. The booming and rumbling sounds were horrific.

I knew it was going to take about twenty minutes or more to get to the location of the woodpile. My concern was a pyroclastic flow, coming down the ravine to the woodpile. If that happened, Brody would be killed.

Yes, I could've headed away from the island like he wanted me to but I could never have gone and left Brody behind. My heart could not deny the fact. I'd rather die with him than to live without him. I started chastising myself, "Why hadn't I told him I loved him sooner? Why did I wait? Why did it take this event, realizing we could die to make me finally say it? May God help me get there and save him."

Finally, I was coming to the area where the woodpile was located. Lava slowly oozing down the slope had much of the jungle and the area of the woodpile nearest the volcano ablaze. The lava oozing from the crack that had formed was flowing into the ocean causing huge steam clouds. The hissing and boiling sounds made by the hot lava hitting the water were incredibly loud.

That's when I saw Brody. He had climbed out to one of the far rocks out in the open water. He was standing there, looking in my direction, waving his hands in the air. He'd taken off his boots and stuck the tops down in his pants with the soles sticking up. His belt was holding them tight against his body. He was not wearing his shirt. I guess he hadn't been able to retrieve it. My heart pounded with joy and I even smiled. Then, I saw him climb down off the rock, ease into the water and start swimming frantically in my direction. I directed the boat toward him.

Reaching the edge of the boat, he grabbed it with both hands. I quickly moved to the far side of the boat to keep it balanced. He pulled himself up and over, landing in the bottom of the boat.

I hurriedly crawled over, grabbing him and kissing his lips and cheeks, "Brody! Brody! I can't live without you! I love you so much!"

Brody looked up and smiled at me, grabbed my head with both hands and kissed me on the mouth, "I love you so much, you silly goose. But we need to get our asses out of here before this thing really blows. When it does, it's NOT going to be pretty." He immediately crawled to the back of the boat, pulled on his boots and grabbed the rudder, turning the boat out into open waters and then to an easterly direction.

"You've got that right! When the ash starts to fall, don't breathe any of it in. You'll end up with Marie's disease which can severely damage your lungs. The ash is full of very fine glass particles and is extremely dangerous. So far, we're lucky the wind is blowing it away from where we are." I happened to be wearing my shirt and quickly removed it, cutting it right down the middle of the back, using the obsidian knife. I crawled over to Brody and wrapped the half section of the shirt, so the upper part of the sleeve went around his mouth and nose. I tied it tightly in the back. "I know this is probably really uncomfortable. But it's made of a material that should make a good filter." I did the same to myself with the other half. "Can you breathe all right?" I asked.

"So far, so good." His voice was a little muffled by the cloth.

"If you feel it slipping off, let me know. I'll tighten it again to keep it over your nose and mouth."

I looked toward the volcano. "When the ash comes, keep your head bent down. Try not to get any in your eyes. It can blind you." I took off my cap and quickly adjusted it for a bigger size and pushed it down on Brody's head. "The visor should help keep the ash out of your eyes."

"What about you?" Brody called out.

"Hey! You're the one driving this thing. It's most important you see where the hell we're going. I can keep my head down. I don't have to see. We've got to get as far away as we can from this place."

Just then, another huge explosion occurred from the volcano. This time, major chunks of rock went flying in all directions. We both were watching and saw a large chunk coming in our direction. I cringed as it got closer. We were lucky. It landed in the water some forty feet behind the boat, causing a huge splash. I looked toward the volcano and saw a pyroclastic flow, coming down the flanks of the cone. "Brody! That's a pyroclastic flow! They're extremely hot and they move like wildfire!"

"Well, we're moving as fast as we can! May God grant us enough speed to get away!" Brody yelled out.

That's when it started. Ash began to fall in big clumps. I got out one of the gold bowls from the front compartment and started scooping it up off the floor of the boat. I also went up and pushed it off the front part of the bow over the front compartment. Brody did the same over the back compartment where he was sitting. I knew it would be heavy and possibly unbalance the boat.

"We can't go to the mainland. If the island blows up, it'll most likely create a tidal wave. Everything on the coastline of the mainland will be wiped away. As much as we may not like it, we're going to have to go through the portal if it shows up."

Brody had a horrible expression in his eyes, "What if it doesn't open?"

I looked at him and shook my head. "Well, in that case, we're up shit's creek without a paddle!"

Brody yelled, "And if it does, what if we end up in that Dinosaur World, you keep talking about!?"

"As much as I hate to say it, it would be the better of two evils! Staying in this time period, we'd be killed by a tidal wave. At least in Dinosaur World, we'd have a running chance. And I do mean running!"

The boat was moving at a pretty good clip northeast and parallel to the shore of the island. We were heading in the direction of the portal in hopes it opened. I continued to scoop ash out of the boat and throw it over the side. I was never more glad I had the boat made as wide as it was. My gyrations around it made virtually no major consequence to its balance. I had to admit that the amount of gold in the bottom was a big factor, keeping it stable as well.

Getting closer to the northern end of the island where our camp was located, we looked out to sea. There was no sign of the portal.

"Damn! It's not open!" Brody yelled out.

"That's all right! Head in the direction where it normally is! If it opens, we'll have to take our chances!"

"Aye, aye, Captain!" Brody headed the boat toward the area of the ocean where the portal always appeared. I kept scooping up falling ash clumps and throwing them overboard. It wasn't easy work but it had to be done and Brody had to stay at the rudder and control the sail.

We were almost two miles away from the island when we heard another enormous explosion and rumbling. Just as it occurred, we saw the portal begin to shimmer and open, virtually right in front of us.

Brody immediately adjusted the sail to maximize the wind. The boat began to move quickly in the direction of the portal.

We both turned and looked toward the island. Another enormous and powerful explosion occurred and the top of the volcanic cone began to slowly collapse inward. Large cracks began to appear on the slopes with molten lava, flowing from them.

Seemingly in no time at all, the boat reached the portal and passed through to the other side. Brody continued to adjust the sail to catch as much wind as possible, taking us farther and farther to the northeast. We knew that even having passed through, we were still in danger. When the tidal wave occurred, it would rush through the portal and into the world where we now were. It was essential to get as far away from the portal as possible.

Interestingly enough, the farther we got from the portal the less ash was falling into the boat. We were about a mile from the portal when we actually could perceive its size and shape. It stretched across the ocean almost a mile in either direction and arched to what looked like about a half-mile high in the middle. It truly was like looking through a giant window. The darkness of the smoke and ash blowing from the volcano made the whole area look as if a huge horrible storm was happening. There was even lightning in the volcanic clouds. We could hear it loudly crack.

That's when we realized we were beyond the limits of the ashfall. The shirt pieces were no longer really needed.

I yelled out, "We no longer need the shirts! There's no ash here!" I went over and untied the one covering his nose and mouth then removed mine.

The boat continued onward for almost twenty minutes. That's when it happened.

With an incredibly horrendous and almost deafening explosion, the whole island seemed to disintegrate and blow into the air. The sound-splitting boom raced in every direction. We could hear it clearly as it rushed through the portal along with several large chunks of rock. We were lucky none of them hit us. It was incredible that the shock wave didn't take down the mast and sail.

The wind was excellent, carrying the boat along at a pretty fast pace. Brody and I couldn't take our eyes off the spectacle, occurring on the other side of the portal. Suddenly, we saw it. Growing in height. Higher and higher it grew.

I yelled out, "Oh, my God! It's the tidal wave!"

Brody immediately went into action. He quickly turned the boat, so the bow was facing the portal and then rapidly lowered the sail. "We have to be facing the wave when it comes through the portal. We may have a chance to ride up and over it that way." Instantly, he was back at the rudder again, holding the boat steady.

"But we're still so close!" I yelled.

"That may be. But we have to be facing the wave. It's our only chance. Damn good thing you had high sides put on this thing."

I'd cleared most of the ash from the bottom of the boat and hurriedly crawled to the back, sitting next to Brody. If I was going to die, I wanted to be with him. It was funny and may sound ridiculous but all of a sudden, a calm came over me. Somehow, whatever was to happen made no difference. Everything was okay.

Turning to look at Brody, I spoke quietly, "Thank you for these past months. You've made me happier than I've ever been with anyone. If it's to end now, I'm glad it's with you. Brody, I love you. I love you so much."

Brody turned his head and smiled, "Thank you for that, silly goose. I feel the same way. But let's not count ourselves out quite yet. You never know."

I nodded my head and started to giggle, "I know it's not funny. But you're right. It's not over… till the fat lady sings."

We watched the wave grow higher and higher and get closer and closer. I couldn't imagine us surviving such a wave. I grabbed hold of Brody and hugged him tightly. He wrapped his arms around me and held me tight as well.

"I love you, Brody."

"I love you, silly goose."

As we watched, the wave got closer and closer. It looked like a huge mountain coming toward us. Suddenly, there was another incredible and deafening explosion.

Just as we thought we were going to be destroyed, unbelievably, we saw the whole area of the portal begin to shimmer. Within seconds, just as the wave was reaching the opening, it closed. The portal was shut. The Fates had been kind. The wave didn't hit us. In the time of the island, it would be traveling toward the mainland. Once there, it would be creating significant damage. Where we were, there wasn't even the slightest hint of a major ripple on the surface of the ocean and the sky was clear as a bell. It was as calm as could be.

Brody gasped, "Oh, my God! It closed! We're saved! Hot damn! How lucky is that?" He grabbed me, hugging me tightly and kissing me. He started to laugh, "Guess it's just not our day to die!"

I hugged Brody. "I don't believe it! I don't believe it! We're still alive!" After a few moments, I stood up, placed my right hand on my chest, the left raised up into the air and started making the singing sounds of 'Ride of the Valkyries' from Wagner's opera.

Brody looked at me strangely.

I stopped singing and grinned as I looked at him, "I did say that it wasn't over till the fat lady sings. Well?" I started laughing.

Brody just bent his head down and shook it. Then, he looked at me. "There's one problem. You're not fat."

We both just roared with laughter.

After a few moments of exhilaration and jubilation, we began to come to our senses again. Now, it became necessary to find out where we were. It was around early afternoon, the sun was bright and we'd have to get our bearings.

Brody looked at me and started snickering, "Okay. Are we now ready to go to Dinosaur World?"

I looked at him and spoke in a scolding manner, "Don't even think it! Geez!"

That moment broke the tension and we both just bent over, laughing so hard even knowing it might be true.

I looked at Brody. "You're covered with globs of ash. It's in your beard and all over your pants."

"I can jump overboard and wash off. And you should see you. Yeah."

"Well, I'd never be able to get back in the boat like you did when I picked you up at the woodpile."

"That's okay. I'll pull you back in the boat. Come around to the back and it won't cause the boat to go off balance when I pull you in." At that, Brody pulled the cap off his head, his boots, jumped over the side next to the boat and swam around in the water. Within minutes he was pretty well washed off. He reached up for the side of the boat as I moved to the other side and seemingly without a problem, pulled himself into the boat. "Okay. Now, it's your turn."

Reluctantly, I responded, "Well, okay." I jumped over the side and thrashed around. I then swam to the back of the boat. Brody stretched across the back compartment, reached down and grabbed me, pulling me onto the back of the boat. Finally, we were back in the boat and ready to continue. "I have to admit. I do feel a lot cleaner." I grabbed my cap and readjusted it again to fit my head and put it on. That's when I realized I had no shirt. "Brody, grab the sunscreen from under your seat. We need to put some on or we'll burn up in this sun." I looked up in the sky toward the sun.

Brody got out a bottle of sunscreen, squeezed some on my back, handed me the bottle and started smearing it around. I squeezed some out and started smearing it on my chest and arms. I squeezed more into my hands and started smearing it all over Brody's back and he started doing his chest and stomach and arms.

"I could get the two pieces of my shirt, shake out the ash and put it on." I looked at the pieces we'd used to cover our mouths and nose.

"Let me wash them out in the water." Brody got them, leaned over the back of the boat and swished each one in the ocean. "I think that works." He handed them to me.

I took one piece and put my arm through it. The breeze caught the front and back and almost blew it off.

Brody began to laugh, "I don't think that's going to work."

"I think you're right. Guess I'll make do with just the sunscreen."

Brody raised the sail, turned the boat toward the mainland and called out, "Okay! Let's head to Dinosaur World!" He looked at me and started to chuckle.

I gave him a scolding expression then started to chuckle as I shook my head. I thought of the old expression. 'It is what it is.' For us, there was no turning back. I truly did hope we were not in Dinosaur World.

"Okay. Okay. I need to get our bearings here." I began to quickly think about it. "Our location should be some twenty maybe twenty-one miles from the mainland."

Brody guided the boat toward the mainland for about an hour. I turned, looking in the direction I expected the shore to be. First, I was looking south. In the haze, I could see the distant mountains far inland. Slowly, I moved my eyes up the coast in a northerly direction. Suddenly, I couldn't believe my eyes. At about ten o'clock, there appeared to be something onshore that was not a natural formation. "Look! Over there! Do you see it!?" I pointed.

"Yes. There's something there. It's hard to see but it looks like some type of construction."

I was shocked and surprised, "That's no construction! I'm pretty sure those are cargo cranes!"

Chapter XIV

"I think those are cranes!" I yelled out again, "I have no idea where we are in time but I have a feeling it's within a few years of when I left. I won't know until we check out the location where the house is supposed to be. If it's not there, we're back in time from before I left. If it's there, there is no telling. But it would be sometime when or after I left."

"Which way?" Brody called out.

I pointed. "That way. It'll take us maybe six or seven hours to get there and it'll most likely be getting dark." I thought of something humorous, "Wouldn't it be funny as all get out to come back and meet myself before I left?"

Brody snickered, "Yeah. That could be a real bitch."

I started to laugh, "Would the REAL Mark Lancaster, please stand up!"

We both roared with laughter.

"Okay! Okay. Let's get serious here. Now, it could also be possible we're way in the future from the time I left and the earth has been taken over by aliens." I knew it was extremely unlikely we were in the future but I just couldn't resist joking with Brody again.

Brody gave a strange look. "Aliens?"

"Yeah. Creatures from outer space. Invaders from Mars." I started laughing.

Brody finally caught the joke and joined in the laughter. He shook his head. "All right already. You're going to have to lead us in. If it's anything like that distance in island time, we've got as you said, at least six hours of sailing yet to go. There is one consolation. It's not Dinosaur World."

I pointed toward the shore and Brody set the boat on course in that direction. After a while, he asked, "Do you think the portal will ever open again now that the island has blown up?"

"That's an interesting question. I doubt it but you never know. The island could possibly rebuild itself like what happened with Krakatoa. It came back again. So, who knows?"

We'd been sailing for over five hours and it was getting to be evening time and getting dark. I estimated it to be around seven-thirty, possibly going on eight o'clock. Continuing to scan up and down the beach, I searched for the house. Suddenly. There it was.

"Brody! Oh, my God! There's the house! The little cove is just south of the house. We can anchor the boat there."

165

Brody maneuvered the boat closer to shore. Before going through the surf, he lowered the sail. Oars in place, he directed the boat right into the cove and near the sandy beach. I was very surprised to see the locking post there. I looked in the top box. There was the lock and key. I showed Brody as he threw out the anchor. We climbed out of the boat and walked up onto the beach that surrounded the cove. The sun was now just below the horizon.

I looked in the direction of the house and saw that the lights were on. I looked at Brody. "Well, this should be very interesting. Especially, when we don't even know what month or year it is here. Under the back compartment of the boat. Get my wallet in the plastic bag. I'm pretty sure there are people at the house and I have a feeling I'm going to need to prove who I am. Oh. And above all, do NOT say anything about the stuff in the boat. Make sure any of the gold plates, pitchers, bowls are hidden in the front or back compartments. No one is to know about any of that stuff."

Immediately, Brody turned, headed back to the boat and got my wallet. Within moments, he was back by my side and handed me the wallet in the plastic bag.

Just then, I saw two people come out of the sliding glass doors and onto the covered terrace. They turned and looked our way. I hoped they were renters and not some new owners. Attempting not to alarm them I called out, "Hello! ¡Hola! How are you? ¿Cómo están?" I wasn't sure where they'd be from, so I thought I'd cover all bases.

The folks on the terrace waved their arms in the air and yelled, "Hey! We're fine! Who are you?"

"Well, unless something major and drastic has happened, I'm the guy who owns this place. Mark Lancaster. May we come up and talk?"

"Really? We were told the owner disappeared." The man spoke as he placed his hands on his hips.

"You are correct. I did disappear. But kinda like in the movie, 'The Shining'. Heeeere's Marky! I'm back!" I started to chuckle, "Sorry. Couldn't resist. Here! It's my wallet. It'll show you who I am." We walked several steps forward and I threw the wallet onto the terrace. "We'll stay right here till you check it out. I swear. We're not drug dealers. Oh. And since it's getting pretty dark if you need more light, there should be a flashlight in the top drawer to the right of the stove. Unless someone has changed everything inside. By the way, where are you from?" I turned to Brody and whispered, "Now, you'll see what a flashlight is."

As the man walked forward to get the wallet, the woman ran into the house. Very shortly, she re-emerged, holding the flashlight in the air. "Either he's a great psychic or he really must be the owner."

The man began to peruse the contents of the wallet. "We're from Atlanta. Came here last August and really liked the place. Never met the owner but loved the online ad for the place. Yeah. Whitby by the Sea. And the pictures were great." He finished looking at the contents of the wallet and called out, "Okay, Mark. I see you check out. Y'all come up here on the terrace. Now, if everyone thinks you disappeared, where the hell have you been?"

Brody turned to me. "You named the house here after the plantation in Virginia. How would you say it? That's COOL?" He slapped me on the back.

"I hope you'll forgive our appearance and the condition of our clothes or lack of them. It's not been easy and today was extremely trying and not kind." Brody and I walked closer to the terrace. "I do have one question. What is today's date?"

The lady spoke, "It's Friday. June thirteenth."

I laughed, "Funny. I left on January thirteenth and now, I return on Friday the thirteenth in June. Instead of it being a bad day." I paused a moment, "Well, it actually has been a very bad day but we survived. So, now, Friday the thirteenth has turned out to be our lucky day. Does anyone see any irony in that?" I shook my head. "What year is it?"

"What year?" She chuckled, "Why, it's two thousand fourteen."

I raised my arms in the air, waving them. "Hallelujah! Thank you, Jesus! Hopefully, I still own the house in Atlanta." Brody and I walked up onto the terrace.

The man walked over and extended his right hand. "Richard. Richard Sanders. This is my wife, Alice."

I shook Richard's hand. "Mark Lancaster. And this is my friend,

Brody Hollister." Brody shook Richard's hand as I turned to Alice. "Hello, Alice." I shook her hand as did Brody.

Richard stretched out his left arm. "Please. Come have a seat. Sit down."

Alice headed over to the wall. "It's really dark. I'll turn on some lights out here." She went and flipped a few switches, lighting the terrace.

Brody's mouth opened, quickly looking all around and his eyes grew big. "Those must be the electric lights you told me about. Wow! That's fantastic."

This was quite perplexing to Richard and Alice. They both looked at one another then turned to me.

"I swear you're not going to believe what I'm about to tell you. I'm sorry we don't have shirts on but I had to use mine earlier today for protection. Brody doesn't have one, either, as it is now lost forever along with the island." I gave a big grin.

Alice smiled, "Just a minute. I'll get you one of Richard's T-shirts. It might be a bit big."

I looked at her. "Look in the bottom drawer in the closet in the main bedroom. I keep a pile of my T-shirts there." I grinned, "If you don't mind getting one of Richard's for Brody, that would be great."

She went into the house. Shortly, she returned and handed me a T-shirt. "Right where you said they were." She handed another one to Brody. "Now, can I get you all something to drink? Iced tea, coffee, orange juice or a cola. If you'd like some of the hard stuff, I'm sure Richard could whip you up a cocktail."

I looked at Brody and he looked at me. We both began to laugh. I shook my head. "I truly would love a cocktail. But, I think I really should stick with a glass of iced tea if that's all right?" I put on the shirt.

Brody smiled, "Mark's right. I should have a glass of iced tea as well." He put on the T-shirt Alice gave him.

Within a few minutes, Alice returned with a tray containing four glasses full of ice and a large pitcher of iced tea. She placed it in the middle of the table on the terrace and we all sat down. She poured the glasses full and handed one to everyone. "I hope you don't mind but it has sugar and lemon in it already."

Brody took a drink but seemingly couldn't stop. Emptying half the glass, he let out a loud sigh, "Oh, my God! That tastes so good! I can't believe how good it tastes!" Brody looked at Alice and Richard. "Please, forgive me. It's just that it's been so long since I've had anything other than water."

I took a drink and virtually did the same thing. "Damn! I'd forgotten how good a glass of iced tea tastes."

Alice laughed, "Well, drink up. There's plenty more where that came from." She shook her head. "Oh, my God, how stupid of me. You guys are probably starving. Let me go fix you something to eat. Is there anything you don't like?"

Brody chuckled, "When you haven't had real food for as long as it's been for me, I have no problem with anything."

I agreed, "Same here. All we've had is fish, guavas, papayas, some limes and some wild pineapple for the last several months. Oh, and a few lobsters when Brody caught some."

Alice got up and went into the house. "Richard, could you come bring some of this stuff out and put it on the table?"

Richard went in and shortly they brought out makings for sandwiches. Alice spoke, "This should be quick and easy for right now." They sat down again. "But don't fill up. I'll fix you something more substantial in a few minutes."

Richard looked back and forth at both of us. "Mark. We heard about you on the news. I think it was back in late January or early February."

"Really? The news?" I started making a sandwich as did Brody. "I have a good friend in Atlanta who works for one of the TV stations. He's one of their reporters."

Richard continued, "Yeah. Back in Atlanta. It was on the local six o'clock evening news for a couple of nights in a row. You worked for a big architectural firm and from what they were indicating, you're one of their top employees. They said you'd come down here on vacation. When you didn't return to work on time, they got extremely concerned and started doing some investigating. After checking, it was obvious you'd gone out sailing since the boat wasn't in the cove and your bike was in the garage. But there was no sign of you or the boat anywhere up and down the coast here. Searches were made but nothing was ever found. They feared you and the boat had gone out and both were lost without a trace."

Richard paused to take a drink of tea, "Now, mind you, we didn't really put all this together till we started realizing the place we'd rented last August, this place, was yours. I'd heard Angelia, your manager here, mention your name several times last year."

"Now, Alice is always looking for whales and dolphins with her binoculars and saw your boat earlier maybe about a mile or so out to sea as it was getting dark. She was shocked because she knew it from seeing it last August. You should've heard her when she realized. She kept yelling out, 'It's him! It's him! And he's coming this way!'" It finally became apparent that she was correct as y'all came into the cove.

"Of course, now realizing the boat belongs to you, I know there's no way you could've gone up or down the coast and not been seen. It's also obvious you didn't just sail out to the southwest to the middle of the ocean, sail around for five months and then come back again. And Brody mentioned drinking only water. There's no place out there in the middle of the ocean to get fresh water. Where the hell have you been all this time? And what's this about an island?"

I looked right at Richard, shook my head and just grinned, "Richard. I swear to God. When I tell you where we've been, you'll look at me and think me insane. No one will ever believe the story. But we almost didn't make it back. When the volcano blew up, I thought we were going to be wiped out by the tidal wave."

A few moments of silence went by before Richard and Alice looked at me very strangely. "When the volcano blew up? Tidal wave?"

Brody nodded with excitement in his voice, "Hell yeah! The sound was deafening when the volcano erupted and blew all to hell."

Alice looked at Brody, questioningly, "When did this happen?"

Brody tilted his head. "Must have been sometime in the afternoon. Maybe around one or two o'clock."

Alice looked at Richard. "Remember that huge loud boom we heard early this afternoon? I thought it might've been some explosion. It really got the chakalakas going. Seems all the groups were squawking together."

Brody interrupted, "You heard one of the explosions?"

Richard looked at both of us very strangely. "Alice likes to use the binoculars. She came out and ran up on the roof after the first loud boom, trying to see what made it. She was sure it had to have been something blowing up like dynamite. She happened to look out to sea."

"Yes." Alice continued, "I noticed something very strange on the horizon. It wasn't very large, probably because it was so far away. It was a dark area. But with the binoculars, I could see it much better. I really couldn't actually make it out but it looked like some very strange storm. And I know this will sound strange but it was shaped like an arch. I swear I saw what looked like flashes of lightning in it.

Then, there came another loud explosion sound and it came from out at sea. I watched it for a while and then suddenly, it seemed to just vanish. Just instantly went away. And the chakalakas were going crazy."

Brody looked at me. "Holy cow! She heard the island blow up and saw the portal! She saw the portal and saw it close!"

"Portal?" Richard questioned, "Okay. I now know we're in for some whopper of a story here but I just happen to think. You need to let people know you've returned. It's going on ten thirty but I'm sure lots of folks would like to know you're still alive."

I started to laugh, "You've got that right. Would you mind terribly if I used your cell phone to call my brother and Angelia? I'm sure mine has run out of service by now. It should be with my laptop. If my laptop is in the top drawer of the dresser in the main bedroom, I can send out a few emails."

Brody leaned over. "Would you mind if I watched? I'd like to see how they work. I'd like to see how the flashlight works, too." He turned to Richard and Alice. "What's a chakalaka?"

Richard and Alice both looked at Brody with a questioning expression. Then, they looked at me. I could read it on their faces. It was obvious they couldn't imagine anyone not knowing about a flashlight, cell phone or laptop and how they worked.

I just smiled, "I'll explain Brody as well. And you're REALLY not going to believe THAT story." I started to chuckle, "Brody. A chakalaka is a bird. It has a long neck and legs and it sounds like a very confused turkey when it makes noise."

Alice laughed, "You've got that right."

Richard got up. "Let me get you the phone and I'll see if your laptop is in the drawer." He went in and shortly returned.

Alice stood up. "I know it's late but I'm going in and make y'all something more to eat. I went to the store earlier today and bought several rib eye steaks. Haven't had time to put all of them in the freezer. How does a steak on the grill sound? Richard can work his magic with his marinade beforehand."

Brody and I doubled over with laughter. Brody shook his head. "Do you know how often we talked about how much we'd both like to have a steak? Thank you. Thank you so much."

Richard smiled, "If you guys want to take a quick shower, please feel free. Mark, you obviously know where everything is. Does Brody have any clothes here? His do look like they're really worse for wear."

I shook my head. "Unfortunately, he doesn't."

"Well, I may have a pair of shorts that might fit him. I'll go check and see." Richard got up and after a few minutes returned with a pair of shorts. "Brody, see if these will fit you."

Brody took the shorts and smiled, "Thank you so much." He headed into the house to take a shower as did I. We both took one at the same time in the main bathroom since the walk-in shower was large enough. I also took a pee and flushed while he was watching just in case he was unfamiliar with the operation of a toilet. I turned to Brody. "And here's the toilet paper, so you can wipe yourself after you take a shit." I pointed to the roll on the holder attached to the vanity. "We don't have to go wash off in the ocean anymore."

I went into the little bathroom closet and looked on one of the shelves. "Yes. There it is." I knew the lady who does the house cleaning always puts my toothbrush, toothpaste and mouthwash in the closet if I should forget to do it myself when I leave to go home after my vacations. It gets them out of the way of renters. There were some extra toothbrushes there, too. Grabbing a new one in a box, I handed the new one to Brody. I also got the toothpaste and mouthwash and placed them on the counter. "Now, we can brush our teeth and gargle with the mouthwash. This is how I do it." I went through the whole process at the sink.

While Brody brushed his teeth, I commented, "While we are here, we will go see my dentist, so she can check out our teeth and give them a good cleaning. Not sure how good dentists were back in eighteen fifty." I chuckled.

Brody almost choked doing the mouthwash but when he finally finished and spit it out in the sink, he smiled, "Wow. My mouth feels like new." He started giggling.

I grinned, "And now when I give you a kiss, I won't have 'Moose Mouth'."

We both broke out laughing as I put everything back in the closet.

Shower over, teeth brushed and in fresh clothes, the next twenty or more minutes I called my brother and then Angelia and apologized for the hour. I didn't go into any details as to what had happened. Both were glad I was still alive. My brother hadn't sold the house in Atlanta. All was well. Brody watched as I called and listened to the voices, coming from out of the phone. He acted like some child who had seen a new toy.

After that, I decided to call my boss from work. I hoped he'd not be too angry at me for calling so incredibly late. When he heard my voice, he was totally shocked. He was so glad I was still around and was hoping I still wanted my job. It made me laugh. He told me to do what I needed to do to get things straightened out and to come back when all was in order. He also said he'd send a few months of my salary to the bank as an advance. He had a feeling I was going to have some possible problems at immigration if my visa had expired and if he could be of any help to let him know.

That's when it hit me. Brody had no visa, no passport. There was nothing in the system about him. As far as the government was concerned, he didn't exist. This was definitely going to be a major problem. We were really going to have to think this one out if Brody was ever to come back to the States with me. And I sure as hell wasn't going to leave him here in Mexico. There was a feeling I was going to have to find some 'special' people to get it to work.

Alice finally called us to the table, "Richard fixed the steaks like medium-rare. If anyone needs them cooked longer, let him know. Not a problem. I also fixed a salad. Here's the Italian and Ranch and Thousand Island dressings."

I snickered, "I think I will pass on the Thousand Island. I've had enough of islands for a while."

Everyone laughed but Richard and Alice didn't get the full humor of the comment.

I'd forgotten how good a steak could be. I took my time eating it to savor every bite. I could tell Brody was doing the same thing. "Richard. Alice. This is amazing. Thank you."

After we ate, Brody excused himself. "I'll be right back." He headed down off the terrace toward the boat. It wasn't long before he returned. He looked at me and tweaked his head, smiling, "I covered the boat in case it should rain. I also locked it on the post there. Here's the key."

"Hang it on the hook by the door over there." I pointed.

Brody did as I asked.

Alice spoke up, "Well, something tells me you two have been through a major ordeal. And as much as we'd love to hear your stories, I have a feeling you both are exhausted. It's even past Richard's and my bedtime. Why don't you sleep in the south bedroom tonight? There are twin beds in there. We can start this again in the morning with breakfast. We're probably going to sleep a bit late tomorrow.

Y'all get up when you like. No rush. Remember. Richard and I are on vacation." She started laughing.

We all laughed.

Alice added, "Oh, Richard and I are headed into town tomorrow after breakfast. I'll get more groceries. If y'all need anything, let me know."

"Alice, thank you so much. I think Brody and I are going to just chill out and get our bearings. Since Richard found my laptop in the drawer, I can send out a few emails. And I swear, I'll have Angelia fix your bill here, regarding the rent."

That really made everyone cheer and clap their hands.

———⁓⁓∘◦◖◗◉◐◗◦∘⁓⁓———

Undressing and getting ready for bed, Brody spoke quietly, "I went out and covered everything with the boat cover. What you said earlier made me realize it was very important for no one to see the stuff in the boat." He sat on the bed across from me, facing me.

"Brody, you're so right. If anyone finds out we have what we do, we'll NEVER see anything of it again. Governments and everyone will forever be fighting over who it belongs to. We'll be left out in the damn cold. I've seen it happen too many times with treasure hunters when they find treasure from lost ships at sea. The damn governments can go fly a kite for all I care. Screw the greedy politicians and officials. We'll sell off the gold little by little, so no one takes notice. The same with the gems. Jewelers will buy the stuff when we say we melted down some old family stuff we had. The bigger stuff I can say has been in the family for lifetimes and is my inheritance. They'll be glad to get it, especially if they don't have to pay top dollar for it. And you know if gems that size had been stolen, they'd have been all over the news. So, questioning them being family heirlooms would be resolved very shortly. Hell, I can get in contact with major jewelers anywhere in the world and send photos of the stuff using my computer. They just might come knocking at our door."

"When Alice and Richard go into town tomorrow, you and I are going to move everything from the boat to the back of the garage. Quickly, we'll have our own buried treasure, using the shovel in the garage. Angelia said Richard and Alice were here for two weeks then no one is renting for a week. If we need to rebury some of the stuff at that time, we will." I smiled, "Remember. When we tell our story tomorrow, no mention of the treasure stuff. But we will keep the big trunk that has a lot of the clothing and blankets in it out for all to see along with the three metal knives and the obsidian one. That stuff along with the logbook will give some credence to the Spanish soldiers."

Brody snickered, "Aye, aye, Captain." He saluted. "Do we tell them everything else?"

"Yep. Everything. Tell them about the cave and the dead Spanish guys in it. The truth will sound so fantastic, they really will have a hard time believing it. That's the way it'll be with everyone who hears it. What's the old saying? 'Truth is stranger than fiction.'"

"And you. You have no paperwork to prove who you are. No passport or visa. Damn. It's going to be fun working something out, so you can come back to the States with me. But there are ways. We'll do it."

I paused for a moment, "But you know? Holy cow! It's so obvious!" I hit my forehead with my right hand. "The truth about you will be so unbelievable! YOU are going to be famous! Trust me. You just might not have a problem doing it legally, open and above board. Historians will be clamoring to talk with you. How often do they get to talk with a man from another century, over a hundred and fifty years ago, before the Civil War? I'll bet some will even go checking to see if they can find out about the ships you sailed on and if there's any record of you anywhere in history. There may even be some old photos from back then with you in them. Geez. Think about it. And if they did, how fantastic it would be for you. It would be proof positive you are who you say you are."

"I have a feeling the folks in the news media will be a huge help. As I mentioned, I know a reporter at one of the TV stations in Atlanta. I'll call him tomorrow. I'll bet he'll even come here to interview us. That'll really get the ball rolling. You never know. And..." I slapped my knee. "The book. The logbook written by the head of the soldiers. We can turn that over and we don't have to worry. There's no mention of any treasure or gold in the book. No one will ever know any existed. Also, there's the volcanic ash in the boat. Volcanologists will prove it so. And we'll have Alice to back up the story with what she saw through the binoculars. We'll talk to her about that tomorrow." I paused for a moment then snickered, "Afta all... Tamarra is anotha day."

Brody looked at me funny.

I shook my head. "'Gone With The Wind'. It's a movie about the 'Recent Unpleasantness'... the Civil 'Wowah'. Yeah. We'll watch the movie one of these days. I have it on DVD back home in Atlanta." I bent my head down and began to giggle, "And I will also show you a couple of episodes of the old TV show, *The Waltons*, so you know about John Boy."

That made us both chuckle.

Brody responded, "Well, if Chester didn't get burned down, my birth should be written in the books at the courthouse there. Who knows?"

"That's terrific. That could be a start. Wow." I paused for a moment, "Oh, my brother said my credit cards should still be fine. No one canceled them. He's also wiring me some money just in case the need arises and I can pick it up in a day or two. We'll go in and get you some clothes and more groceries. I didn't want Alice to know I could go tomorrow because I wanted that time for us to bury everything. The sooner, the better. Out of sight, out of mind."

"Other than that, we're alive and well. The next few months, I feel are going to be VERY interesting. VERY interesting. For me, it'll soon be back to business as usual. After we sell off some of the gold, I can reimburse my boss for the advances he's going to put in my bank account. For you? For you, I hope you'll adjust and I'm sure you will because, for you, it's going to be a brave new world. What can I say? And as we slowly dispose of our find and convert it to cash and investments, I may consider taking early retirement. Very early." I chuckled then paused for a few moments. I smiled at Brody, "And Brody, I'll try and help you adjust to this new world. Just know... I love you."

Brody looked back at me and smiled, "I think I'll be just fine." He gave a huge grin, "I love you, too, you silly goose."

We both stood up and hugged each other tightly. Our future was going to be bright and filled with love.

———∿∿∿∿———

Meanwhile, deep beneath the surface of the sea, some twenty-five miles offshore and in some mysterious unknown time, lava was slowly flowing from cracks in the sea bed. The island of the portal was beginning to rebuild.

The End

Printed in the United States
by Baker & Taylor Publisher Services